Estrella Paints Gargoyles

A Novella in Episodes

By Doctor. G.

Estrella Paints Gargoyles available on Kindle Vella.
Read first 10 Episodes Free.
Google: Kindle Vella. Enter Title. Read.

Conscious Books
316 California Ave., Ste. 210
Reno, Nevada 89509
U.S.A.

ISBN 978-0-9619917-7-7

Cover Image AI Generated

Book Design: Ankit Todi – Fiverr

Email: spiritualfrequenciesonline@gmail.com

Instagram: drgfrequencies

X: @FrequenciesDrG

YouTube: Greg Nielsen@DrG1

Additional digital books, video and audio including the *Tuning In* podcast go to:
Patreon.com/spiritiualfrequencies

Venmo: contribute directly to Conscious Books and Spiritual Frequencies Online Academy: @Greg-Nielsen 9

Other Books by Doctor G.

Minnehaha Falls

Star Consciousness: Direct, Maintain and
Transform Your Energy

Gateway to Stardust: How to Resonate with
Natural Order Frequencies

RiverSpeak (poetry)

Tuning to the Spiritual Frequencies
(with Light Wave poems)

Beyond Pendulum Power
Pendulum Power
Pyramid Power

Additional online books:
Patreon.com/spiritualfrequencies

Episode 1

My name is Señor. That's what Estrella calls me. I met Estrella in Segovia, Spain while studying Spanish at San Juan University in Madrid. We developed an unlikely friendship which resonated a deep connection. After I returned to the United States, we nurtured our friendship by email, Facebook, Instagram, TikTok, WhatsApp, Skype, and FaceTime. We were inseparable in the virtual world.

As Spanish summer school conversation partners in Madrid, I learned that Estrella dreamed of moving to New York City to pursue her art adventure. I lived in Bar Harbor but lived in NYC for twelve years before moving to Maine. She wanted to know everything about the city. In many ways it was like Madrid but bigger. She especially wanted to know about the art scene. I didn't know anything about the art scene.

I heard a notification ding. It was five am. I was not awake nor was I asleep. I rolled over, stretched slightly and glanced at an eager phone.

"Are you up?"

I debated. Up or not up? Up. I knew Estrella was flying from Madrid to NYC today. I was flying to NYC from Portland, only an hour flight, to meet her.

"I'm up." I texted back,

FaceTime. I answered.

"I can't wait," exploding with enthusiasm.

Dressed in a pastel blue blouse and matching pastel blue casual pants, Estrella was raring to go. She wore the rose quartz necklace I gave her for her birthday. I could see her bedroom window behind her. It was raining. She lived above the plaza where the Roman Aqueduct of Segovia survived millennia. I wondered if the aqueduct still carried the rainwater.

"I'll be at the airport when you land," I said confidently.

"Thank you Señor."

"Does the rainwater still flow along the aqueduct?"

"Yes, isn't it amazing it still carries the water?"

"Can you see the water flowing from your window?"

"Here, I'll show you."

Estrella scooted over to the window turning the phone toward the aqueduct below. The water rushed in a torrent. It was amazing. I wondered where it flowed. Before I could get a chance to ask, Estrella flopped her suitcases up on the bed.

"Got to go. Mom is calling me down to the car. Papa must stay and run the café."

"Okay, adios amiga."

"Adios."

I had to get going myself. I still needed to pack and do a bunch of errands before making the hour drive to the Bangor airport. Estrella's cousin Luna lived in New York City, in the borough of Brooklyn. Estrella was going to live with Luna. Luna couldn't make it to the airport since she was on a business trip to Los Angeles.

I packed for a long weekend. I loved autumn in New York. I was staying with Billy, an old friend who I hung out with when I lived in New York. Luna was flying in on the red eye from LA arriving early in the morning. I promised to keep Estrella company until Luna made it home.

Episode 2

We landed at John F. Kennedy airport early, about 5:30 pm. Estrella's plane was expected to arrive about 6 pm. I exited the plane and looked at the flight arrival-departure display. Estrella's flight was now expected to arrive about 6:30 pm. I made my way to the international flight terminal after I stopped to fill up my water bottle at a touchless dispenser.

JFK airport is humongous. It was more than a hop, skip and a jump to the international terminal. I walked at least a mile. Arriving, I checked my phone for the time, 6:20. I found a seat outside of customs and texted Billy.

'Estrella's flight is about to arrive. You might want to head this way.'

'Ok dude, I'm on my way.'

Billy lived in Brooklyn Heights not far from Luna. He wanted to time his trip to JFK so that he didn't have to drive in endless circles around the arrival loop. I wondered how Estrella would do in NYC. Segovia is a small rural city. Yeah, she went to university in Madrid which gave some preparation for NYC. Still, at heart she was a small-town girl.

Being a writer, I'm always observing. The hustle-bustle of people crisscrossing felt like a psychic overload coming from the peace and quiet of Bar Harbor, Maine. I maxed out on the NYC intensity after twelve years. I needed a more contemplative environment in order to write.

I took a sip of water. The custom doors opened. I got up and moved closer to the doors.

I hadn't seen Estrella for more than two years. She graduated from the University San Juan Carlos, had three art openings in Madrid and got her own apartment, art studio in Segovia. She worked at the family café to pay the bills.

My anticipation made it feel like a long time before she wandered out of customs. I waved my hand. She smiled. We met up with a warm, friendly hug. I could tell she was both excited and anxious.

The drive to Brooklyn Heights swarmed with cars buzzing in and out. Billy buzzed like an angry wasp. Estrella and I talked non-stop, some in English and some in Spanish. Billy parked in front of Luna's apartment. She lived on the third floor of a brownstone just off Court Street. Billy and I each grabbed a large suitcase.

"Does Luna have a roommate?"

"No, I don't think so."

"How are we going to get in?"

"She said there was a hide-a-key magnetic key box underneath the fire extinguisher in the hall." We lugged the massive suitcases up the stairs. Billy huffed and puffed while I just huffed. We searched high and low for the fire extinguisher with no luck.

"Are you sure she said it was on the same floor as her apartment," I probed.

"I just assumed it was," responded Estrella.

"I'll be right back." Billy was done and Estrella had travel fatigue.

I went on a search down to the second floor, then to the ground floor. I found it. It was in the hallway leading down to the basement. I rubbed my hands along the top, bottom of sides of the extinguisher until I felt the hide-a-key box. The climb back up was easy without the massive suitcase.

Entering the apartment, it was obvious Luna made the big bucks. You can't live alone in NYC without roommates unless you're making at least a quarter mil. The furniture was new and expensive. There were mirrors in every room. We gave ourselves the grand tour. There were two bedrooms. The larger one was her bedroom; the smaller one was her office.

Episode 3

We sat down on Luna's custom-made turquoise couch. We were all exhausted and hungry. We didn't even have energy for small talk. Estrella looked out of place. Welcome to NYC. She got up and went to the window. She gazed at the panoramic view of New York harbor with the Statue of Liberty center stage.

"Billy, you can go," I suggested. He fidgeted trying to find a comfortable spot on the massive couch. "I can get a cab or Uber to your place."

"Thanks man. I've got shit to do. I'll see you later. Nice meeting you Estrella. Welcome to the Big Apple."

Estrella gave me a look, 'Big Apple?' With a knowing glance I let her know I'd explain later.

"Thanks for the ride Billy," Estrella said politely.

Billy nodded and left. Estrella seemed out of place. It was all so new and strange. I was starving. I went into the kitchen and opened the refrigerator. It was filled with SmartWater and not much else. I grabbed two bottles.

"I'm exhausted," Estrella declared. "Please don't leave me alone. Stay here until Luna arrives."

"Okay." I handed Estrella a water. "Are you hungry?"

"Si, tengo hambre."

"Siri, what are the closest restaurants?" A list came up. I gave my phone to Estrella. "Do you see anything you would like? We can order and have it delivered."

"Pizza, American pizza," she said with a burst of energy.

We ate pizza, drank smart water and attempted to watch tv on the seventy-inch screen. I couldn't figure out the controls, so we listened to music on the XM radio app. We fell asleep on the massive turquoise couch.

We woke up to the jarring sound of the apartment door opening. Luna burst into the apartment dressed in all pink, even her Converse shoes were pink. Behind her was the taxi driver lugging two large suitcases.

"Estrella, Estrella, Estrella, wake up." She pointed to the bedroom indicating the driver to put her suitcases there. She had her smartphone in one hand and a twenty-dollar bill in the other. She handed the twenty to the driver as he left. There was no thank you.

Luna waltzed around the living room taking one selfie after the other using her well placed mirrors. "Get up Estrella. We need to take some photos. We need to post them." She barely gave me a glance. I wondered where she got all her energy. She flew all night.

Luna played her smartphone like a Stradivarius violin tapping out the words and uploading the selfies in rapid fire. "Come on Estrella. Over here." Estrella struggled toward Luna. Luna placed her arm around her and took a barrage of photos.

I sipped some smart water and planned my escape. I texted Billy who lived only ten minutes away asking him to pick me up. Luna and Estrella spoke Spanish so fast my ear could only make out a word here and there. I thought it odd that Luna never acknowledged me, not a word or a glance.

"Hasta Luego, see you later."

"Adios Señor," Estrella said with heartfelt sincerity.

Episode 4

Estrella bought a shit load of art supplies at the Court Street Art Store. Paints, brushes canvases and an easel. She hauled them back to Luna's place. Luna gave her a key. She climbed the stairs and entered the apartment. She laid the supplies on the floor and looked for Luna.

Estrella quietly entered Luna's office. She was mad at work on her laptop interspersed with staccato actions on her smartphone.

"Sorry to bother you. You said you had a workspace for me. I want to start painting. Where should I set up?"

"When I said I had a workspace, this is it. It's my office. This is where I do most of my work."

"What do you do?"

"I'm the social media person for Upbeat, a music video company." Luna dressed the part, monochromatic. Today she wore royal purple. "You can set up in that corner."

Estrella grimaced slightly. She imagined a massive artist space. She had seen photos of NYC artist lofts with high ceilings and giant windows. Stuffing her easel in the corner would cramp her style. She liked it quiet with no distractions. Luna was a like a ping pong ball.

While awkwardly setting up in the corner, Luna received a call. She talked incessantly about Instagram, Tik Tok, Facebook and YouTube. Estrella doubted she could create in such an environment. She needed peace and quiet.

The apartment doorbell rang. "That's Alan." "Alan?"

"You'll love him. One of my boyfriends."

Luna unlocked and opened the door. Alan plunged into the apartment embracing Luna with a splash. There was no introducing. Alan only noticed Luna. They headed to the bedroom and closed the door. Estrella felt out of place, lonely. She sipped smart water. She longed for connection. In Segovia she had family, friends and community. Luna wasn't like the family she hoped for.

Estrella set up her corner of Luna's office to paint. It was cramped. Her creative energy was blocked by anxiety. She felt like calling Señor. She assumed he was back in Maine writing. She called him Señor from the first time they met in the family café in Segovia. She hesitated. She couldn't make up her mind.

She left the apartment and explored the Brooklyn Heights neighborhood. She walked toward New York Harbor. She strolled along the promenade bordering the East River. She doubted her decision to move to NYC. The skyline inspired with a panoramic wonder. She sat down on a newly painted bench. She FaceTimed Señor.

"Hola, mi amiga."

"Hola, Señor."

"How's it going?"

"Maybe I made a mistake moving here."

"Estrella, it's only been a day. You've got to give it some time. Give yourself at least a month and then see how you feel."

"Luna isn't really like family."

"Yeah, I noticed. She's lives in her mirrors. Maybe you'll need to find another place to live in order to be paint."

Episode 5

I originally met Estrella after wandering into a small café off the Roman aqueduct plaza in Segovia, Spain. The hot, dry Spanish summer made me thirsty. The café air showered me with cool air. I sat carefully on a kind of bar stool. There was a row of 7 stools. I sat at the end stool.

I craved water as I picked up a menu. It was in Spanish.

"Señor."

Looking up, I witnessed stunning beauty. My spine shivered with electricity. I believed I had seen many beautiful women. This server across the counter was the essence of beauty created in another dimension. Her face luminated. Her beauty was more than physical. Her energy felt like meditation. I gasped while my heart skipped several beats.

"Señor?"

I hesitated, mesmerized. I tried not to stare as I peered into radiating green eyes. I was a beginning Spanish speaker. I traveled to Madrid for the summer to learn Spanish at Universidad de Juan Carlos. I managed a reply.

"Hola, señorita. Aqua, por favor." She quickly realized I was not a native speaker.

"Esta bien."

She moved fluidly for a glass of water, a lucid dream. The heightened awareness exhilarated me. Her luminosity glowed with moonlight. I grounded myself on the café stool. She returned with the water.

"What's your name?" I asked with an American accent that must have been laughable.

"Estrella."

Star in English. I was gazing at a star. "Do you speak English?"

"I speak a little, un poco."

I pointed to the menu. "I will look," I said self-consciously.

She understood and left allowing me space to decide. I seemed to be the only one who recognized Estrella's presence. Remarkably, no one else noticed. They had to be regulars. Let me assure you my attraction was not the male gaze. Oh, no! This was about angel energy. She touched me inwardly.

Previously I had met a couple of evolved human beings who emanated uplifting vibrations. In their presence, what they call in India darshan, you know they are not every day run of the mill humans. There was Francois in New York City and the yogi in Fort Collins, Colorado.

I could not concentrate on the menu, so I settled on ordering a coke. My appetite had disappeared. I mostly wanted to revel, savor the moment. She was a server, an everyday regular working person with an angelic vibration.

Estrella returned to take my order. She wasn't rushed. She was calm and positive.

"Coke, por favor."

"Esta bien. Un momento."

Here I was in Segovia, Spain; the Roman aqueduct was not the attraction. There was Estrella. She was the attraction, a joy. Even the Alcazar castle, the inspiration for the Disneyland castle, was no comparison.

Episode 6

There was no way we were going to have a long-term connection. I was on a day trip from Madrid with my classmates. By 5 pm we would be on the hour and a half bus trip back to the University San Juan Carlos.

Estrella smiled as she put the coke on the counter. She asked me where I was from. I told her I was from America studying Spanish in Madrid. She complemented me on my Spanish. That was nice of her. The truth was I was very much a beginner. I could not hold more than a two or three-minute conversation. My vocabulary was no muy grande.

It was frustrating to meet someone like Estrella and not be able to communicate. I wondered how she became the way she was. Did she grow up with her radiant presence since birth?

Were her parents like her? I thought maybe she was a devote Catholic who truly lived a spiritual life. At least on this day I did not detect anything dark. I wondered if she was like this all the time or was she just having a really good day.

I finished the coke, paid Estrella and left the café. Walking across the aqueduct plaza I kept thinking of her. I couldn't get her out of my mind. Keeping her in my thoughts somehow kept us connected. It was a special experience. I was no longer a tourist in Segovia. The quality of her being gave me a new experience that changed my life forever. Perhaps I missed it before. Perhaps I just didn't notice. I happened onto someone remarkable.

That's how we met. Clearly, Estrella was distraught. Luna displayed little or no thoughtfulness or understanding for Estrella's artistic dream. She really didn't want to return to Luna's apartment especially with her boyfriend there. One day in NYC and she wondered if she had made a big mistake. At least in Madrid she had galleries who showed her work.

"Estrella did you bring your laptop?"

"Yes," she responded with curiosity.

"You have your smart phone with you, right?"

"Si."

"Ask Siri, what is the closest artist coop to my presentation location?"

Estrella asked in English.

Siri responded, "Please use Spanish."

Estrella asked in Spanish. Meanwhile, Señor Googled on his laptop entering 'what is the nearest artist coop in Brooklyn Heights, New York'?

Siri responded to Estrella, 'since you are in New York City change your language setting to English.'

"Señor, I'm getting nothing."

Señor piped in, "Court Street Art Store. It's only a couple of blocks from you."

"I was there this morning buying art supplies. I know where it is."

"Okay, go there right now and ask them where you can get studio space. And ask about sharing an apartment with artists."

"Great, I will."

"Call me later and let me know what happened."

"Gracias Señor."

"De nada. Adios."

Luna had the right name alright, Luna for lunatic. By far Estrella was more beautiful inside and out than Luna. Estrella's natural auric energy emanated beauty without effort. Luna did everything outwardly to cast a superficial spell of Instagram beauty. I thought that in a way Estrella was lucky she had to deal with Luna. Online, digital media was rampant with Luna phony boloney.

Episode 7

The Court Street Art Store had a network of artists they shared with Estrella. They suggested three that she should contact since they had shared living artist lofts. She headed back to Luna's place to make some calls. Estrella entered the apartment hearing Luna's voice chattering away in the office. Estrella poked her head into the office. Luna did not acknowledge her. There was no nod or hand wave. She just kept talking while continually looking into the wall mirrors.

Estrella set herself up on the turquoise couch and dialed the first number. The assistant manager at the art store warned her that often people do not answer their phones and that it might be better to text first and introduce herself. As predicted, there was no answer. Maryanne was the contact's name. Estrella entered the contact into her phone.

'Hi Maryanne, my name is Estrella. I'm an artist from Spain looking for a place to live and paint. I got your name from The Court Street Art Store. I'd love to meet and see your loft. If you have any time today, I can stop by.'

Estrella waited for a few minutes hoping for a speedy reply. Nothing. She moved on and sent a text to the other two contacts. She felt anxious. Her mind raced with thoughts that she had made a big mistake coming to New York City. On the other hand, she did not want to return to Segovia. She knew there was no future for her there as an artist. Family and friends would not understand her chosen theme, painting gargoyles.

I know when I first saw her paintings at the art studio at the Universidad de San Juan Carlos I was stunned by the gargoyles. It seemed incongruous. At first glance gargoyles are ugly, horrific, demonic. Estrella is beautiful, calming and angelic. The contrast disturbed by sensibilities.

Estrella grew up in Segovia. Segovia is a family values, Catholic town. Most attend church every Sunday in a Gothic cathedral. Estrella's parents gave her every opportunity especially since she had no siblings. That's surprising since Catholics tend to have at least three children. My guess is that there was some sort of complication.

Estrella was an outstanding student earning top grades all the way through high school. From an early age she loved to paint. Segovia is surrounded by farm country. Her aunt and uncle owned a farm nearby where she spent lots of time during summer vacation. She liked all the farm animals and loved to paint them.

When she turned thirteen, she worked during the summer and after school at the family business, a small café on the aqueduct plaza. Tourists from all over Spain, Europe and all over the world poured into Segovia during the summer months. Estrella worked long hours. She had little time to go to the farm or do things with her friends.

She learned a lot about people, and she made a lot of money. She saved her tips, amounting to over one hundred thousand Euro by the time she moved to NYC. She had no time to spend it since her parents provided everything for her.

You can imagine her parents weren't too happy about Estrella moving to NYC. They missed her when she went to college in Madrid. They always believed she would move back to Segovia after graduation and settle down. To them it meant she would meet and marry a good Catholic boy and have a family. When her parents retired, she and her husband would take over the café.

Episode 8

Estrella received a text. 'Give me a call. We may have space for you, Maria.' Estrella immediately called Maria. The loft was only a few blocks away. Maria invited her over immediately. Reaching a large brick warehouse building, Estrella entered the dimly lit lobby and took the industrial elevator to the fifth floor.

Maria warmly greeted Estrella. They exchanged hellos while Estrella scanned the large open space. She felt at home seeing the easels, canvases, and tubes of paint. The large windows invited light into the creative artists' haven.

"How many artists live here," inquired Estrella.

"Four. We have room for one more."

"Are you all painters?"

"No, two of us are painters and the other two do pottery and sculpture." Estrella could not wait to move in. After reviewing the rent and utility costs, Estrella was ready to move like now, today. The rent was double the rent for a similar space in Madrid. But Estrella didn't care. There was no way she could live with Luna.

"Can I move in today," Estrella asked with enthusiasm.

"You will need to meet the other three. I can't just let you move without their okay. Can you come back about 6?"

"Yes, I'll be here." Estrella didn't want to spend another night at Luna's. Besides, she wanted to paint. She came to NYC to paint not to socialize or deal with a crazy cousin.

Estrella entered Luna's apartment. She could hear Luna talking in her office. Estrella poked her head into the office. Luna barely acknowledged her giving a slight nod. Estrella wanted to gather her art supplies, anticipating the move to the artist's loft. They were not there.

"Where are my art supplies?" Estrella asked with a burst of anger. Luna did not respond. She really didn't even hear Estrella. "Luna, I want to know where you put my art supplies," she asked just shy of yell.

"I've got to go. I'll text you later. My cousin needs something." Luna actually looked at Estrella. "What it is?"

"My art supplies, where are they?"

"I put them in the front closet. They cluttered up my office."

Estrella did not respond. She went to the closet, opened it and looked. Everything was there. She carefully removed everything and stacked her supplies by the apartment door. She was going to move as soon as possible, tonight would not be too soon. She went to the bedroom and shut her suitcases. She hadn't unpacked them. She lugged them to the front door.

Luna floated out of her office videoing her legs and feet while peering into the mirrors.

"Do you want to go to Chill tonight with Alan and me? We're doing Molly."

"I found an artist loft cooperative nearby. I'm moving over there."

"Moving? You haven't even moved in here." Luna wanted to show off her cousin from Spain to her friends. Estrella was a kind of status symbol.

Luna would be even cooler having an artist cousin from Madrid.

"I need a lot more space to work than you have here. I'm moving this evening."

Luna went about her business uploading her latest selfie video to Instagram and Facebook.

Episode 9

Estrella had a couple of hours to kill before 6. She decided to take a walk along the Brooklyn Heights Promenade. The view of the Manhattan skyline from the Promenade inspired. And then there was the East River and the Brooklyn Bridge and in the harbor to the west The Statue of Liberty. Freedom was why Estrella moved to NYC. The freedom to be who she wanted to be meant creating, painting what she wanted to paint.

Strolling north along the Promenade, Estrella's thoughts flowed into a creative current. She glanced at the skyscraper skyline across the river. She didn't know which skyscraper was which but looked forward to picking them out by name someday. Many of them had figures adorning upper stories. She wanted to paint these figures like she painted the gargoyle figures on the gothic cathedral in Segovia.

The fall air was crisp and invigorating. Estrella decided to sit on one of the many benches lining the Promenade for nearly a mile. She felt free, libertad. She people watched. Americans strolled along with other nationalities.

Estrella travelled in a daydream. She saw the colors, held the brush and felt the canvas coming alive. She loved the huge south facing windows at the loft. Tomorrow would be an all-day paint day. Estrella's magnificent daydream was interrupted from time to time by guys gawking. She appreciated her physical appearance good fortune but at the same time wished she was invisible.

The Uber car pulled up to the artist loft building. He kindly assisted Estrella unloading the suitcases. Estrella took a sip of water as she pushed the intercom.

"Yes," Estrella assumed it was Maria.

"It's Estrella." The buzz. Estrella opened the door, loaded everything on the elevator and pushed four.

Maria greeted Estrella and introduced the other artists. Maria didn't say anything about bringing all her stuff. After all she hadn't been accepted yet into the fold.

Maria introduced Sylvia the potter and Brad and Ellen the painters. Maria was the sculptor. They all sat down in a living room seating area with two well-worn couches and a few wooden chairs. The floor and walls were concrete. The windows filled the room with evening light.

"We want to let you know up front that it's a one-year lease. We are firm on that. The rent is fifteen hundred a month with two months deposit. We split the utilities five ways. It's due on the twenty fifth so you need to Venmo me by the twentieth." Maria was all business, no fluff.

"Tells us about yourself," Brad interjected with a skeptical tone.

"I graduated from the University of San Juan Carlos in Madrid with a degree in art. I've painted since I'm thirteen."

"Do you have a portfolio?" Brad cut to the chase.

"Yes." Estrella opened her portfolio and hand it to Brad.

"Looks like you only paint gargoyles. I hope you don't expect to have any showings with only gargoyle paintings."

"I had three showings in Madrid."

Episode 10

Tall, lean and chiseled, twenty-five-year-old Brad glowed Adonis. Most women dripped with obsessive attraction. Friends with benefits, Brad and Ellen competed for top painting honors. Maria and Sylvia thought he'd look great in a dress and high heels. Brad knew he could have any woman he wanted. It repulsed Estrella. Many Spanish men were that way.

According to the Swiss psychologist, women project their ideal male image on a man. It has a vibrational power that he called the numinosity of the archetype. Ladies read *She: Understanding Feminine Psychology* by Dr. Robert A. Johnson. It's a smorgasbord for thought.

"I vote no," barked Brad. Maria, Ellen and Sylvia votes meant zero since they agreed a new roomie vote had to be unanimous.

"How about you Maria?" Estrella asked desperately.

"Sorry Estrella. We need to vote unanimous for a new roommate.

"What am I going to do?" asked Estrella anxiously.

"Take your stuff and leave," Brad stung while taking a sip from a bottled water.

"I'll ask around," Maria interjected trying to take the sting out. "You might want to go back to the art store and ask.

Dejected, Estrella piled her suitcases and art supplies on the elevator. Maria and Sylvia gave her helping hands. Down she went, down into depression. Estrella couldn't go back to Luna's. Estrella dragged her stuff outside. The sun was dropping behind the skyscrapers. A cool rain started falling mixing with a thick polluted air.

"Hi Estrella, que pasa?"

"I have nowhere to do my art Señor." Estrella turned on FaceTime.

"Looks like you're out on the streets. You didn't get the artist loft apartment?"

"I can't go back to loco Luna's."

"I'll call you back in a few. I'm going to have Billy pick you up. Hasta pronto. What's your address?"

Estrella sat as close to the building as she could to not get wet. She didn't have an umbrella. Fortunately, the rain was not a downpour. Despair washed over her. America, the home of the brave and the land of the free, was turning out to be a nightmare not a dream come true.

Señor called back. "Billy is on his way. How come you didn't get the loft?"

"One of the artists voted against me. He said there was no way I'd make it in New York City."

Estrella heard a voice shouting from above. It was Maria leaning out a window.

"Estrella, wait. I'll be right down."

"What is it?" asked Señor.

"It's Maria. The woman I first met about the loft. She's coming down. I'll let you know what happens."

Estrella waited anxiously. She wondered if she forgot something. Maybe Maria was bringing it down. Billy lived a couple miles away. He pulled up to the curb just as Maria came outside.

"We got Brad to change his mind. But you'll need to sign a one-year lease. Okay?"

Billy got out of the car.

"Yes, a one-year lease is great. Thanks Billy. I don't think I'll need your help. Sorry. It looks like I'm moving in."

Episode 11

"Thanks Maria."

"Don't thank me; thank the landlord. We reminded Brad that rents were going sky high, and we may not survive another rent hike. Then we would all have to move out and move to Maine."

"Thank you for reminding him."

Estrella's corner of the loft felt joyful and happy. It was furnished with a double bed, an old wooden dresser, a rack to hang clothes and best of all huge windows. She made herself at home. New York City, her dream, was coming true. She drank from a bottled water. She had no food. She didn't need it. She had a creative life.

Exhausted from jet lag, the Luna insanity and the no place to create, Estrella slept. She dreamt of light and color and paint. She dreamt of Spain. She dreamt of artistic success. She dreamt of gargoyles on gothic cathedrals during monsoon rains. Torrential rains drained from the gargoyle mouths.

The light cascading through the massive windows pierced Estrella's closed eyes. She welcomed the light. She was energized by the light. Even though she had to pee a river the first thing she did was set up her easel.

There's was activity in the loft. She didn't know where everyone slept and worked. They didn't give her the grand tour of the loft except to show her the one bathroom. The bathroom door was closed. Estrella needed to pee right now. She knocked on the door.

"I'll be right out," barked Brad.

Brad burst from the bathroom like a war hero. He said nothing. There was no smile, nothing. Estrella wondered why he was so cold, heartless. The pee dam broke. Relief. Now a hunger plague gripped her belly.

She made her way to the open kitchen area. Sylvia and Ellen sipped coffee.

"Coffee?" offered Sylvia.

Estrella hesitated. She wasn't sure what the American etiquette was in this situation. She had served tens of thousands of cups of coffee in the family café in Segovia. Coffee wasn't her favorite, but she wanted to fit in, and she wanted to know her roommates. What she really wanted was some food, and a cortado

"Sure, thank you."

Ellen poured her a mug full. The mug was a one of kind.

"Did you make this mug? It's a beauty." Estrella asked Sylvia.

"No, it's Ellen's handywork. I'm the sculptor.

Estrella took a sip. It delighted her. It wasn't acidic like the Segovia café coffee.

"Do you want a half a bagel?" Sylvia sensed Estrella's hunger.

"Tengo hambre. I'm starving. Where can I buy some food?"

"There's a grocery store about four blocks away. We are going there this afternoon if you want to come along," offered Sylvia.

"The large refrigerator is ours. The two small ones are Brad's and Maria's. We suggest you buy your own frig. It will save a lot of conflicts. No one borrows food unless you ask," Ellen clarified.

"Thank you,"

Famished, Estrella consumed the toasted half-bagel and cream cheese. She wanted to paint. She came to NYC to paint. It was time. She laid out her supplies, paints and brushes on a small table next to her easel. She had purchased three small canvases from the art supply store to get her started. The morning light irradiated the canvas. She decided to paint a gargoyle she had painted many times before. It was inspired by the gargoyles from the Segovia Gothic Cathedral.

Episode 12

When Estrella painted, time evaporated into thin air. Expressing creative energy feels like a direct line into a joyful, happy world. The day-to-day demands diminish in favor of spontaneous flow and serendipity. Life is good. Who has time for worries and troubles? Estrella didn't have brothers and sisters. She had creativity.

We had creativity in common. When she talked about how she felt when painting, I understood even though I'm not a painter. I'm a writer. When I write my consciousness accelerates into another timeless dimension. Everything is more alive, brighter. People and things radiate a luminescence.

Remember when you were a kid. Finger painting, scribbling, drawing outside the lines, building sandcastles and playing the flutophone –

the list goes on and on – all were playful, unselfconscious creativity. Estrella and I would sometimes ask: what happened? Where did the fun go, the play, the natural creative energy flow? We didn't know for sure. But something happened between about twelve and fourteen or so.

Estrella told me her parents met when they sang in the choir at the Gothic Cathedral of Segovia. They were seven or eight. They loved singing in the choir. It made them happy and free. They continued to sing in the choir until they graduated high school. About thirteen singing in the choir seemed more like a requirement than fun. By sixteen singing in the choir was what the choir master wanted not what they enjoyed.

The morning light scintillated across the canvas. Cloud movements changed the light from shade to shade. Estrella loved to paint gargoyles when the sky was overcast. Rainy days were best. Gargoyles loved the rain. They came alive in a downpour. The draining torrents rushed like a mighty river in spring shooting out of their gaping mouths. Estrella cast a pink brushstroke across the gargoyle's body.

"What's up your hotness?" Brad flirted. "Gargoyles will never sell, not in this market."

Estrella did not respond. She kept on painting. She had been hit on by brain dead men since she was thirteen. Working as a server at her parent's café she'd seen and heard it all. Men from France, Italy, Greece, Spain, Germany, Austria, America, Brazil ... have waved their magic wands of male testosterone dust. When she was thirteen, fourteen, fifteen she was flattered. Now, nothing.

Brad usually got a women's attention with his flirtations. He was one good looking dude. He had mojo, sexual magnetism. He wasn't used to being ignored. He would need to do a lot better than a few meaningless flirtatious words.

"Coffee?" Brad offered.

"No thanks. I've got my water."

"If you want to break into this market, I suggest you paint flowers, giant flowers."

Estrella paused letting time pass. Besides she was deeply into the creative flow of her first NYC painting.

"Brad leave Estrella alone. Can't you see she's busy?" Maria admonished. "You know the loft policy, no hitting on each other. I'll take you up on the coffee."

Estrella took a deep breath. She was glad that it was over. She knew it was coming. Most men can't help themselves. They have to test the waters. In a way, she felt sorry for their thoughtless compulsion. Too bad Brad couldn't offer some encouragement. As a painter himself he more than likely had some insights that Estrella would welcome.

The morning disappeared in a puff of smoke. Creative magic. She felt free. Inspiration bubbled to the surface as she painted.

Episode 13

Estrella settled into a routine. Paint, eat, drink water, sleep. She had no time for a social life outside the loft. She loved to walk along the promenade where the trees on one side were red, orange and yellow autumn and on the other side soared the Manhattan cityscape. In between flowed the lazy East River feeding New York Harbor.

Her daily walk was really a walking meditation. Her mind bubbled with creative ideas. She paid attention to the faces, the city moods and the energies she felt. Morning walks pierced her skin with fall to winter air. Afternoon walks warmed her face. Night walks were dream walks with a billion city lights.

Estrella stretched her canvases into larger and larger squares and rectangles. The loft felt free with light and ceilings ten feet tall. Estrella kept to herself. From time-to-time Maria would stop by Estrella's corner studio. She'd look and smile. She could tell Estrella didn't really want to be disturbed, interrupted with small talk. Estrella would respond with a happy glance.

The only person Estrella talked with for the first month was Señor. At night, Estrella often felt lonely. She missed her amigos, her familia, her Segovia. She wondered about her artistic future. Who would give her a showing? Who would buy her art? Would she survive as an artist in NYC?

I never called Estrella. I knew to wait for her call. She knew she could call me day or night, twenty-four seven. Sometimes I'd be asleep. Sometimes I'd be writing. I was on deadline for my new book. The manuscript was due by Halloween.

The phone rang waking me from a deep, dream sleep. It was 2 a.m.

"Señor, did I wake you up?"

"Oh, no. You know I don't sleep. Who needs sleep? I see you don't need any."

"When are you coming to the city?" ignoring his playful sarcasm.

Señor relieved his dry mouth with a sip of water while glancing at the digital clock.

"At the end of October. In fact, I meet with my publisher on Halloween."

"Let's meet up. I need a tour of the city. Remember you said you'd show me Central Park?"

"Do they celebrate Halloween in Spain?"

"Yeah, we celebrate for three days to your one."

"I know what you're going to go dressed as," boasted Señor.

"You know me too well. Do they trick or treat in the Big Apple?"

"You live in New York City for less than a month and you already call it the Big Apple."

"Yes, they trick or treat. It's not like the suburbs where kids go door to door. Usually, there's a massive party, a fiesta somewhere."

"Let's make plans. Are you staying with Billy?"

"Yep."

"What are you going to dress up as?"

"I haven't given it any thought."

"Well, give it some thought. El Dia de los Muertos is our biggest day, November 2. How long are you staying? There must Spaniards living here."

"I'll give it some thought."

"Bye Señor."

Estrella sat in the dark. Only the glow from her smart phone screen dimly, briefly lit her loft corner.

Episode 14

Estrella painted and painted and painted. She soared in the creative skies. The days blinked by. The canvases stacked up against the cement walls. Estrella felt it was time to show her latest works.

She had no idea where to show or how to show in NYC. She showed regularly at university. She had her own show her senior year. Her art professor had contacts in Madrid where she had a show.

Profesora Sanchez was a godsend. She encouraged rather than criticize or overly critique. Estrella's creative confidence grew over the years at Universidad de San Juan Carlos. Growing up in Segovia Estrella kept her gargoyle paintings hidden. Her parents and friends would not understand. She painted more traditional images of Segovia Street scenes and countryside landscapes that were acceptable beauty.

From time-to-time Ellen stopped by to see what Estrella was painting. Estrella and Ellen both painted but did not really connect much. Ellen painted giant flowers in vibrant colors. She was going strong in the NYC art scene. Her paintings were hanging in the homes of the rich and famous and in mostly new commercial office buildings.

Ellen didn't know what to make of the gargoyles. One day Ellen stopped by Estrella's loft corner.

"What do you think?" asked Estrella. "Really, what's your opinion? Maria told me you have an agent who sets up showings."

"I don't know. I really haven't formed an opinion yet. Our painting subjects are so very different. I do admire your dedication."

"How do I get a show?"

"I wish I knew what to tell you. Everyone finds their own path. I lucked out by bumping into an agent at a Manhattan nightclub. Before that whatever I tried led to a dead end."

"What about Brad? Do you think he could give me some pointers, probed Estrella?"

"As I'm sure you noticed, Brad is not a big fan of your art. Besides, he's not one to help any other painters. He is easily threated by other artists. He's never acknowledged my work and he's never come to any of my Manhattan gallery openings."

"Has he had any significant shows?"

"Not yet. Still, he has a showing almost every month. They're mostly in smaller venues like coffee houses and restaurants. He has developed a following. He sells his work, but it doesn't support him yet."

"How does he pay the rent?"

"He's a waiter at a fine dining restaurant."

"That's why he comes home late at night," realized Estrella. "I need to look at his work."

"Good luck. He's very private. He's not like you. You leave your work out in the open. He keeps his work covered with the front of the paintings turned toward the wall."

"You've never gone to one of his openings?"

"He doesn't invite us. But he does have a website, bradwilson.com and all the social media. I'd say the best way to get a gallery interested in your work is to set up a website and post on Instagram. Most galleries don't take appointments where you can show your portfolio. It's too bad. Visiting a gallery in person can be much more effective. Create a website; start posting on Instagram. That's my best advice."

"I will. Thank you."

"You're welcome to come to my next opening. You never know who you you'll meet."

Episode 15

Estrella felt cooped up. She realized she hadn't been out of the loft for nearly two weeks other than to buy food and bottled water. She loved water. She drank it all day long. Growing up in Segovia with the Roman aqueduct outside her bedroom window gave her an ever-present meditation on water.

It was time to emerge from the painting dimension, the creative universe of joy and timelessness. It had been weeks since she had her favorite morning drink, a cortado, espresso with steamed milk. Maria told her that the best coffee in Brooklyn Heights was at Blue Sunrise on Court Street.

It was only a five-minute walk. Entering Blue Sunrise Cafe burst in a vision of Navy-blue merch - barista's aprons, jeans, t-shirts and hoodies.

She ordered a cortado, sat down and waited for it to be delivered to her table. Two men sat nearby. She could feel they were talking about her. She was familiar with how men viewed a pretty woman from working in the Segovia Café. The attention felt uncomfortable. It took way from the full enjoyment of sipping a cortado.

She ignored the vibrational discomfort. It was obvious one of them was working up the courage to come over. She was careful not to make eye contact. That would offer encouragement. Fortunately, the barista who brought the cortado blocked their view.

"I hope you enjoy," the barista said genuinely.

Estrella picked up the cortado and sipped. It was a delight.

"It's perfect. Thank you."

To make herself look busy Estrella took out her smartphone. She just wanted to enjoy the cortado. She pretended to check email and text messages.

It dawned on her to do a search for a Day of Dead event in the NYC Hispanic community.

Fantastica! She came across the NYC Spooktacular Ball on November 2.

The two dudes left. The cortado tasted even better. She scanned the Blue Sunrise Café. The décor was light, airy, bright in contrast with the pop out Navy-blue clothing worn by the baristas. She wanted one of the t-shirts. She wanted to paint in it. She liked that there were no slogans or logos on the t-shirts. They only had the name of the barista.

"Can I get my name on the t-shirt?" enquired Estrella.

"When you buy two or more, we will get your name on the t-shirt," replied Miguel.

"I'll take two. When will they be ready?"

"In two days."

"Do you work mornings?"

"Yes, Tuesday through Saturday from six to eleven."

"I'll see you in two days."

Estrella paid, thanked Miguel and headed back to the loft. I sent her a text letting her know I was coming to NYC on the day before Halloween. I invited her to come along to my publisher, then we could visit Central Park and maybe do lunch at the Guggenheim.

Estrella texted back about the Spooktacular Ball letting me know I needed to bring my costume. I had no idea what or who I would be. I wasn't into Halloween, but I decided to give it my all since we were going to a Spanish speaking celebration.

Estrella worked on her costume between painting marathons. She wanted it to be spooky perfect. She returned to Blue Sunrise for the cortado every morning always ordering from Miguel. She loved the t-shirts. Wearing it while painting did something magical. The fabric felt warm and soft. The color accelerated her creative mood.

Episode 16

A giant neon sign flashed in alternating pumpkin orange and blood red. It read InterNations NYC Spooktacular Ball. Estrella dressed as a gargoyle, all black with a singular stripe of hot pink. My costume was less imaginative. I doubt anyone knew who I was.

I had a somewhat obsessive fascination with the story of Rip Van Winkle. Looking it up on Wikipedia it read: "Rip Van Winkle is a short story by the American author Washington Irving, first published in 1819. It follows a Dutch American villager in colonial America named Rip Van Winkle who meets a mysterious Dutchmen, imbibes their liquor and falls asleep in the Catskill Mountains."

He falls asleep for twenty years and wakes up with a long gray beard. I dressed like an early nineteenth century colonial sporting a long gray beard. We got a lot of stares as we entered the ballroom. The gawks were compounded by Billy dressed as the Humpback of Notre Dame. The mask was horrifically ugly not to mention the huge, deformed hunch.

There had to be a thousand in the giant ballroom celebrating Day of the Dead, Dia de los Muertos. In Spanish speaking countries it is usually celebrated on November 1 or 2. It's a continuation of Halloween. Supposedly there were mostly Spanish speaking attendees.

Estrella assumed the hunchback was Billy. We circulated and mingled. Many spoke Spanish. We stood in line until we each had a skull glass of blood red punch. Estrella struck up a conversation with one of the punch servers. I could make out most of conversation. The server was from Columbia, and she worked at the United Nations.

Next, we headed to the tapas bar with a smorgasbord of Spanish delights. We each filled a plate and sat down listening to flamenco guitar. If you're not familiar with it check it out on YouTube.

A woman with elaborate make up walked up to us. She was accompanied by a man dressed as Bruce Lee. She acted like she knew us. She looked directly at Estrella.

"Hi Estrella." Estrella peered, not recognizing who it was. She took a double take. "It's me, Luna. So great to see you here."

"Luna?" Estrella was baffled.

"Yeah, it's me. This is Jason, one of my boyfriends." Jason nodded. "Where are you living? I texted you a couple of times and I tried finding you on Instagram."

"How did you know it was me?"

"Who else is going to come as a gargoyle? The whole family knows you paint gargoyles."

"Including my parents?"

"They might be the only ones who don't know. Or maybe it is more accurate to say they just don't believe it."

"This is Señor and Billy."

"Come on, let's get a photo of us. I need to post on my Instagram." Luna insisted. "You know I have more than a million followers. Give me your Instagram username. Mine is LunaTikTok."

Estrella got up and took a cousin selfie. Luna jetted off with Jason.

"You might want to follow Luna on Instagram. It might help your art career," encouraged Señor.

Episode 17

Bumping into Luna was a surprise. It made Estrella realize she needed to do more of what Luna did. Marketing and social media was not her forte. She painted everyday which was rewarding and energizing. If she was going to make it in NYC she needed to show and sell her work. She needed a following. She decided to meet up with Luna and ask for her help.

As the evening hours met midnight the music changed from flamingo guitar to spooky sounds, hard rock and gangster rap. They say birds of feather flock together. Señor, Billy and Estrella were morning people not all-night partiers. They simultaneously agreed it was time to go home.

On the way back to Brooklyn Heights Señor and Billy chatted about Billy's work. Estrella realized she knew next to nothing about Billy. It turns out he counselled students at a Brooklyn high school. Mostly he advised seniors on what choices they had after graduation.

Billy wasn't a big talker. In fact, he didn't say much of anything. She found out he was on winter break. He was single and liked to travel to Southern California in the summertime. He had friends and family there. I met Billy at my first book signing.

Riding the industrial elevator up to the loft in the early morning felt creepy. Entering the loft, Estrella heard some activity in the kitchen. She spotted Brad as she headed to her cozy corner. Brad didn't say hello, not even an acknowledging nod. After more than a month she and Brad hadn't had any kind of connecting conversation.

Exhausted, Estrella got ready for bed and snuggled under the covers. She reflected on what she wanted to paint in the morning and that she needed to get the word out about her painting. She knew she needed help. Returning to Segovia was not an option. She knew NYC was her creative destiny.

Estrella drew inspiration from her dreams. The images, sounds, people, symbols, animals had numinosity. She always had a dream journal handy. Many times she wrote them down. Many times she remembered but didn't write them down. The morning after the Day of Dead she wrote the dream down.

There were skyscrapers soaring into a star filled sky. She couldn't tell if they were NYC skyscrapers or somewhere else in this world or another. She saw gargoyles moving from building to building like a dancing parade. She felt anxious but not afraid. The gargoyles were almost life-like yet solid stone at the same time. Crowds gathered pointing to the gargoyles. Fear, laughing and admiration filled the crowd.

Estrella wondered what it meant. It felt positive but she didn't know how to interpret it. As we walked through Central Park, she told me the dream. I had no idea what it meant. I suggested she meditate on it or perhaps paint the dream. She liked the idea of painting the dream.

Central Park in November was bone cold especially if there was a Northeast wind. She asked me about my new book. I hadn't shared much with here.

"What's the title?"

"We don't' have a title yet. But I have a working title, *Center Time*."

"What's that mean?"

"To me, *Center Time* is about sharing experience with the best words I can muster."

Estrella asked me to think of connections I might have in the NYC art world. It could be a friend of a friend. Perhaps my publisher might know someone. Maybe it was one of my avid readers.

Episode 18

Estrella fell into a deep morning ritual. If she remembered her dream, she wrote it down. After that she imagined what she was going to paint. Then she got dressed and went to Blue Sunrise Café for a cortado. She only ordered from Miguel. He knew exactly how Estrella liked her cortado.

Finishing the cortado, Estrella walked back to the loft the long way. She loved the promenade along the river. She began to recognize some of the same morning walkers. No one said hi but there were slight smiles and an eye twinkle of recognition.

Estrella painted until about noon. By then she was starving. The hunger fought against the creative flow. Often the creative flow out dueled the hunger until another hour passed. When that happened Estrella ate whatever she had on hand.

A cracker and Manchego sheep cheese was the staple. She usually did not eat a lot but just enough to keep the life fire going.

After a meager lunch, Estrella devoted at least an hour to marketing her painting. She set up an Instagram account and posted photos from showings in Madrid. She followed Luna's Instagram @LunaTicToc. Luna had a huge following of more than a million, a lot for someone not famous.

One afternoon while reviewing the website being created by a Fiverr website designer, Ellen stopped in Estrella's corner of the loft. Estrella knew almost nothing about Ellen other than she was a painter too.

"How are you doing?" asked Ellen awkwardly, even timidly.

"All good. How's *your* painting Ellen?" Ellen didn't answer Estrella's question.

"Maria told me you're looking to show your work. There's a Brooklyn Heights artist showing for painters the week before Christmas. Brad and I show every year. You can show two works. If you're interested, I'll tell the organizers."

"Yes, please. I really appreciate it. What do you think I should charge?"

"It's up to you. It's hard to say."

"Take a look. What do you recommend?"

Ellen viewed two gargoyle paintings leaning up against the cement wall. She didn't seem to react either positive or negative. She wasn't awe struck or dumbfounded. She seemed non-judgmental.

"I really don't know," Ellen answered honestly.

"What do you charge?" Estrella probed.

"Keep in mind the gallery gets half. You need to let them know by tomorrow so they can include you in the marketing."

"Good timing. My website will be up and running tomorrow."

"Excuse me. I've got to go." Ellen said while leaving abruptly.

"Ellen, who do I contact?"

"I'll text you the number."

Estrella was beside herself with anticipation. It was a small showing, but it was a start. She wondered how Brad would feel about it. He seemed more of an adversary than an advocate.

Brad never gave Estrella the time of day. Estrella wasn't sure if he was threatened, highly competitive or just a 10 on the asshole meter.

The rest of that afternoon Estrella debated on which two paintings she was going to show.

Episode 19

Estrella decided to paint two new paintings after seeing the gallery wall space. She wanted to stand out but also fit in. She spent the next month painting for her first opening in NYC.

She was the first one scheduled to hang her paintings in the holiday show. This meant she did not get a preview of the other artist's works. The gallery director gave her two paintings a nod and a wink while saying, "Different."

Estrella FaceTimed me.

"You're coming to the opening, right?"

"You know I would not miss it for the world. I might miss it for another planet."

"Very funny. Be sure to bring Billy."

"Who else? You might consider inviting LunaTicTok."

"I don't know; she's her own show. It might distract from me and the other painters."

"Are your roomies showing?"

"Yes, Ellen and Brad."

"Have you seen what they are showing?"

"No, we have a kind of creator's code in the loft. We don't really look at each other's work unless we just happened to walk by or catch a glance."

"Who's coming to the showing?"

"As far as I know it's gallery regulars. It's an annual holiday show."

"I looked at your website. Impressive. I noticed you didn't use gargoyle in your domain name."

"Yeah, I was going to, but my web designer said it could narrow my audience."

"And you never know, at some point you might branch out and paint other images. What if a patron gave you a commission to paint something other than a gargoyle but still using your style, would you do it?"

Estrella paused. She wasn't sure. It was a great question.

"I guess it depends. We would need to agree on the image. We would need to discuss it."

"Yeah, that sounds wise. You can always say no or suggest something else. Of course, they may just say here is the space, go ahead and paint what you want."

"You'll be there?"

"I said I'd be there. I'm not going to miss your first New York City show." Estrella and Señor said their goodbye.

Estrella planned, sketched, imagined, dreamed and painted day and night. All her passion, time, energy, know-how and creativity went into the two paintings. She had gargoyles on the brain. She lived on cortados, snacks and bottled water. The days sped by like comets. She lived in another dimension where time gave way to a timeless now.

She hardly socialized with her roommates. Maria understood. Brad didn't know that Estrella was preparing for the same showing and Ellen didn't tell him. Estrella could tell that Sylvia wondered what was going on. She never asked, keeping to her pottery making. Pottery sales were big during the holidays.

With just a day to go, Estrella obsessed on the touch up colors. She stared endlessly at her creations waiting for an inspiration. Lighten here, darken there. No doubt, she knew this was her best work. The gargoyles came alive with dream-like movements.

Episode 20

Estrella experienced a toss and turn night. She kept thinking and thinking and thinking until she was exhausted. She wished she could stop thinking. The more she thought about stopping thinking the more the thinking persisted.

Finally, she got up and walked quietly around the loft. The only light was in the kitchen. The thoughts came in tsunamis. She racked her brain. She worried she might have forgot something. She hoped the gallery patrons would like her work. She wondered if anyone would buy her work. Did she give the paintings an affordable price? What would the other artists think of her paintings?

Walking around the loft settled her thoughts. Drained and mentally spent, Estrella sat on her bed gazing out the window at the lower

Manhattan skyline. In the distance, somewhere over New Jersey she spotted airplane lights. She figured they were headed to Boston or coming in for a landing at Newark airport. Exhausted, she lay down and melded into a dream sleep.

Estrella slept until the loft was filled with sunshine. Usually, she woke up before sunrise. She had no plans to paint. She dressed, snuck out of the loft and headed for Blue Sunrise for a her daily cortado.

"There you are," greeted Miguel.

"I couldn't get to sleep last night," explained Estrella. "Are you coming to the show?"

"I'll be there," Miguel assured Estrella as he hustled up the cortado.

"Make that a double today, Miguel."

"You got it. By the way, I told our owner about you. She wants to display local artists next year. I told her I'd report to her about tonight's gallery opening."

Estrella didn't respond but she managed a furtive smile.

Señor and Billy waited for Estrella inside the front entrance of the gallery. They arrived a few minutes early. Señor knew how punctual Estrella was. They didn't want to view her paintings before she arrived.

Estrella entered greeting Señor and Billy with hugs. Her smile shined.

"Thank you for coming."

"We wouldn't miss your first NYC opening," Billy jumped in.

"Give us the tour," Señor said with genuine enthusiasm.

"This way." Estrella pointed toward the back of the gallery.

There were already ten or fifteen viewing the art, sipping wine and chatting. Entering the back, Estrella looked at the bare white wall. Shock and terror shot through her. What? Crazy! An empty wall space appeared like a white hole. Her paintings were gone.

Dumbfounded, Estrella froze. On either side of the white hole there were two Ellen paintings and two Brad paintings. Ellen and Brad were nowhere to be seen. Estrella managed to turn to Señor. She could not speak.

"They took down your paintings? There must be an explanation. Let's talk with the gallery director. Billy, you stay with Estrella. I'll find the gallery director."

"Señor will sort this out," reassured Billy.

Señor searched the front of the gallery by the wine table.

"Red or white," asked a woman who seemed in charge?

Señor asked, "Are you the gallery director?"

"Yes, do you want to buy a piece?"

"My friend's paintings are missing. They are not on the wall."

"What? That's not possible. I did a walk through an hour ago and everything was perfect."

Episode 21

Estrella retreated into an anxiety bubble. Thoughts whirled in a tornado of thoughts. Who removed her paintings? Maybe the gallery director decided they didn't fit. Perhaps the other artists voted her work removed. Did someone steal her art? She couldn't pull herself out of a psychological negative vortex.

"Estrella, Estrella," repeated Señor attempting to poke through the bubble of despair. "The Gallery director is looking into it. She's asking around the gallery. She said if she must, she will check the security cameras."

Dumbfounded, Estrella heard garbled and muffled words. She felt like she was in a sound tunnel with the sounds at one end and she was standing at the other. Señor did his best to get Estrella's attention.

The gallery filled with patrons. They swarmed around her and Señor. Estrella's name and painting reference were still on the wall. They read: *Enlightened Gargoyles*, Estrella. Patrons stopped and looked at the empty space on snow white walls. Some acted like the white space was the art. Others looked puzzled. Some figured the paintings hadn't been hung yet.

What seemed like hours rather than minutes the gallery director returned. Billy also returned having done his own search. Señor waited for the verdict. Devasted, Estrella just wanted to go home.

"Nothing," reported the gallery director.

"Billy?" anxiously asked Señor.

"I looked outside, outback and in the front. I even searched the dumpster. Nothing."

"As soon as the showing is over, I will check the security cameras," assured the gallery director.

Estrella wanted to respond with a genuine thank you but was still speechless. Señor responds for her. "Thank you."

"Billy, let's get Estrella out of here."

Arriving at the loft, Estrella regained her speech.

"Thanks guys. Please come in. I don't really want to be alone right now."

"I got to get up early. Got work tomorrow," Billy gingerly stated since he really wanted to stay and be supportive.

"Señor?" Estrella hoped.

"I'm with you Estrella," Señor assured. "See you later Billy. I'll get an Uber to your place later."

Estrella and Señor entered the loft. Maria sat in the common area sipping tea. Ellen and Brad were nowhere to be seen.

"How was the opening?" Maria asked enthusiastically.

"Not so good. Maria, this is Señor. I've told you about him."

"Hi Señor." Señor nodded acknowledging.

"What happened? Maria asked with urgency.

"Someone removed or stole my pieces."

"What? That's insane. Sit down. I'll make you some tea." Maria moves to the nearby kitchen area.

"Señor, what do you think happened?"

"No idea. I've never heard of anything like this. Your paintings are not small. Someone must have seen something."

Episode 22

Estrella didn't feel like talking. She sat numb. I felt her need to be quiet in her mixture of despair, fear, anger and the desperate unknown. My mind wandered. I realized in some fateful way it would turn out for the best. Maria returned with a pot of tea and filled our teacups.

We all sat in silence sipping tea. Maria and I respected Estrella's painful silence. We both avoided the bullshit speech about a positive outcome. Somehow it was all for the best. Who wants to hear that when your soul has been crushed by unexpected life.

Estrella did not touch her tea. Maria and I sipped until our cups were empty. Finally, Estrella came out of her self-imposed trance.

"Señor, do you want to see my loft space?"

"That be great."

Estrella rose from the common area couch, picked up her cold tea and led the way. Her loft space was in the back. Estrella flipped the switch lighting the high ceiling, cement walls and giant windows.

Shock quivered through Estrella's nervous system. Against the wall were the two missing paintings. Estrella and Señor simultaneously thought, 'What the Fuck.' Estrella's mind raced through a list of her roommates. Obviously, it had to be one of them.

Maria, no. Sylvia, no. It had to be either Ellen or Brad. Why would Ellen tell her about the showing then remove her paintings. That made no sense. It had to be Brad. That made sense.

"It had to be my roommate Brad," deduced Estrella.

"Señor please don't leave until Brad comes home. I don't want to face him alone."

"Sure, of course." Señor paused embracing a long silence. It was a minute or so, but it seemed like ten. "What if he doesn't come home?"

"He'll come home. He likes to be the alpha. I expect he'll have some justification."

Señor nodded in support. He carried a notebook in his back pocket and a pen in his eyeglass case. It was clear that Estrella did not want to make small talk. She was agitated. She was understandably angry but more stunned that someone would be so cruel. My brain rained ideas on my new writing project.

I glanced at Estrella now and then over the next hour. Her mind spun like water down a drain. I'm sure you all know what I mean. You just can't stop it. You think about what you're going to say in a hundred different ways. You question: is it best to attack or to listen? Or do you just say nothing and let them say something first. The possibilities are endless.

More than an hour passed. I was getting tired. I thought about walking back to Estrella's studio and really looking at her two paintings. Afterall, I came down to NYC from Maine to support Estrella and enjoy her creativity. I could tell by glancing at her that she wasn't into it, so I let it go. Eyes drooping, I got the feeling that Brad wasn't coming home anytime soon.

Estrella, exhausted with stress, dozed off. Somehow, I stayed awake wanting to be somewhat alert when Brad came home. We had never met. I already decided I wasn't going to be the mercenary friend who takes up psychological arms. This was Estrella's battle.

Midnight came and went. I gave up forcing myself to stay awake. I fell into an ocean sleep. But as I did, I gave myself the suggestion to keep an ear out for the sound of the loft door opening. The metallic unlocking mechanics triggered my internal alarm. My head shot up.

Episode 23

I expected a man; it was a woman. Estrella remained fast asleep. The woman was more shocked to see me than I her. I quickly introduced myself. I purposely didn't whisper speaking in a regular voice. I hoped Estrella would wake up.

"I'm Señor, Estrella's writer friend from Maine. You must be Ellen."

"Oh, yeah. She talks about you often." Ellen sees Estrella asleep, walks over to her and gently gives her a shake.

"Estrella." Estrella pops up with a jolt gathering her bearings. "We didn't see you at the showing. Where were your paintings?"

"Where's Brad?"

"He went with friends after the opening."

"He removed my paintings and brought them back here. There in my studio."

"No way. The gallery director kept things hush hush. She didn't really want to spread the word that your paintings were missing or stolen." Estrella rarely got mad. She was volcanic. Brad had to know Estrella was going to rage against him.

"Ellen, there's no way I can live here with Brad sabotaging my work. We need to have a roommate meeting. I'm moving out as soon as possible." Señor stayed out of it. He supported Estrella but didn't want to fight in her battles. Ellen wisely suggested Estrella sleep on it.

"Let's sleep on it. We can meet tomorrow and get to the bottom this. Brad often stays out late after an opening."

"I agree with Ellen. Let cooler heads prevail." Señor texted Uber. "Call me tomorrow."

Reluctantly, Estrella agreed. Still, her mind was made up. One way or the other she was not living in the loft anymore.

Estrella peered at her two show paintings for several minutes before going to bed. She loved the colors – black, grey, dark blue with a light stroke of yellow. The gargoyles were clearly formed with gaping mouths. They were ominous but not evil. They weren't friendly to be sure. But they weren't about to attack either. Their eyes were protective like guard dogs.

Estrella's sleep was far from sound. She was half asleep all night. She kept imagining the front loft door opening and Brad arriving with a devil may care attitude. From the moment they met Brad wanted nothing to do with Estrella.

Estrella really didn't care about getting to know Brad. She had no inclination to get to know him. With most people she felt a natural human curiosity to connect on some level but not with Brad. Mostly she tried to stay out of his way.

Waking up, Estrella thought about a cortado at Blue Sunrise. Her outlook about the show improved. Afterall, she could bring the paintings back to the gallery and hang them again. Of course, it would have been great to have them at the show. Still, they would have a month run at the gallery.

Miguel waved as Estrella entered. He went into barista action creating a perfect cortado. "Where were you last night? The gallery buzzed with rumors that your art was stolen."

"No, my roommate took them down and brought them back to the loft."

"He sounds crazy. Why?"

"I don't know. I haven't talked with him yet.
What I do know is I'm not living there anymore.
I'm looking for another place. If you hear of
anything let me know."

"I'll ask around. We get a lot of artists
coming in."

Estrella took her cortado to her favorite
table looking out on Court Street.

Episode 24

Estrella sipped a perfect cortado. She decided to move to Manhattan. That's where the creative action radiated to the world. FaceTime, she assumed it was Señor. Surprisingly, it was Luna. Luna dressed in a montage of pink. Even her hair was streaked pink.

"I heard your paintings were stolen."

"That's what we thought at first. It turned out Brad, one of my loft mates, took them down and brought them back to the loft."

"That's what I'm calling about. I'm moving to Manhattan, in the Village. Our company bought the penthouse floor of the renovated Hotel Allen. They're looking for tenants."

"I'm in. When can I see the space?"

"I'll text you the address."

"Got to go."

"Luna, thank you so much for letting me know." Luna already hung up. She missed the thank you.

Estrella's phone rang FaceTime. Simultaneously, she got Luna's text with the contact number. It was Señor.

"What happened? What did Brad have to say?"

"I haven't seen him. He never returned to the loft."

"What are you going to do?"

"I'm moving. There's no way I can live around someone who undermines my art."

"Do you have any idea where you want to move?"

"Yeah, the Village, in the old Hotel Allen."

"That's where I lived when I first moved to New York. I hear they have renovated it."

"Yeah. Will you go with me to see it?"

"Of course. The Allen goes way back. I think it was built in the nineteenth century. Artists, writers, musicians, dancers ... creative people have lived in The Allen. I believe Jackson Pollack and Andy Warhol used to live there."

"Really? Incredible."

"When I lived there it was a dump but affordable for a struggling writer. You could hear mice running around at night. The bathroom was down the hall. I had to buy a pair of plyers to turn on the water for the shower."

"Luna's company bought the penthouse floor. She says there's space for an artist."

"It's in the heart of The Village. You'll fit right it. I hope you can afford it."

"As soon as I have a time to look at it, I'll get back to you."

"Okay. Adios."

Estrella finished her cortado and speed walked back to the loft. She knew she needed to talk with Maria about getting out of the lease. Her mind walked faster than her feet. She imagined a creative explosion with patrons buying her gargoyle paintings. She knew it was her time. She could feel the flow. She would have her own creative space.

Entering the loft, Estrella searched out Maria. She was sculpting in deep concentration. Estrella didn't want to interrupt startling her out of her creative flow. Estrella knocked on the wall just inside Maria's artistic cocoon. Maria did not respond. Estrella knocked again.

"What is it?" Maria sharply responded. She turned seeing Estrella quickly changing her feeling to one of compassion. Ellen filled her in on the gallery drama. It wasn't going to be pretty with Brad.

Episode 25

"Sorry to bother you but we have a bit of a crisis." Estrella got right to the point.

"We best have a roommate meeting as soon as possible," responded Maria.

"I'm giving my notice. There's no way I can paint here with Brad sabotaging. I found a place in The Village. I'm moving the first of the month."

"O – K."

"I'll keep paying my rent until you find someone else."

"I'll organize a meeting tonight. I believe Brad is off tonight."

"Thanks Maria."

Estrella left Maria to her sculpting. She felt obligated to spend time with Señor since he came to The City for her opening. She called the real estate agent setting up a walk through that afternoon.

Estrella and Señor took the subway to 14th street and walked to Hotel Allen on 10th. They met up with the agent in the lobby and took the elevator to the penthouse floor. The agent unlocked the door. Estrella eagerly entered into the space.

"It's a one bedroom with a living room space that you can use as an artist's studio. Luna told me you're a painter. The windows are on the south so there's lots of sunshine."

Luna didn't hear a word the agent said. She moved into an imagination reverie. She imagined this exact space when going to university in Madrid. She knew she would be prolific and successful in this artist's apartment.

"I'll take it," interrupted Estrella.

"Don't you want to know how much?"

"I'll take it."

They left Hotel Allen and walked to Washington Square Park just a few blocks south. Along the way they stopped for coffee. Estrella ordered a cortado. She needed to find a cortado as good as the cortado at Blue Sunrise in Brooklyn

Heights. I ordered a coffee black. We sat down on a park bench and sipped our coffee.

"How's the cortado?"

"It's okay. Not as good as the cortado Miguel makes."

"The Village has a coffee shop on almost every block."

The sounds of many drums from the other side of the park permeated the air. We could still hear each other talk. At first, we didn't say much. We took in the sights and sounds. We were bundled up, wore gloves and beanies and sipped hot coffee.

"I'm heading back to Bar Harbor the day after tomorrow. Do you want to ride the Staten Island Ferry tomorrow?"

"Yeah, we haven't done that. Yes, let's do it. What are you doing tonight?"

"Billy and I are hanging out. You're welcome to stop by. Maybe we could go out to eat. Billy says he knows a good restaurant."

"I don't know. I better deal with the roommate situation. I still have not met up with Brad. More than likely we will have a meeting tonight. I doubt I can get out of the lease so I may be paying double rent for a while."

"Do you have enough money?"

"Right now, I do."

The drumbeats, the warm sun, the leafless trees and the people coming and going felt comfortable. I could feel Estrella's calm joy. This was her new barrio, her neighborhood. Have you ever met someone who seemed to be flowing with their destiny?

Episode 26

Estrella painted all day. She was naturally high on creative energy. Taking a break, she Googled "NYC Gargoyles." She came across an article titled *New York City's Spookiest Building Gargoyles* by Andrew Littlefield. Several NYC buildings with gargoyles included The Woolworth Building, The Chrysler Building and Hotel Allen.

'What? No way, Hotel Allen?' thought Estrella. She focused on the Hotel Allen gargoyle photos. Apparently, in the building renovation the six gargoyles were restored. Over the years, from wear and tear, gargoyle pieces fell to the sidewalk below.

She realized that only in few feet away from her new apartment were gargoyles. She wondered if they directed water away from the building. She knew she needed to paint them and the other NYC building gargoyles as part of a show. The inspiration vibrated through her. Her spine tingled.

Estrella sent me the link. This paragraph stood out.

"Sculptors in the city, back in the 19th and early 20th century, often had lots of freedom to carve what they wanted," says John Gill, author of the 2017 novel, *The Gargoyle Hunters.* "On more humble buildings, the architects didn't design the ornaments, they would just write the word 'carving' on the plan. On the worksite, the stone would already be set into the building. The carver would trot up to the worksite and foreman would point to the keystone and say, 'Give me a Moses!' and that meant the carver could carve any imposing face he felt like – himself, his father-in-law or his bartender."

The cornerstone on the 10th Street entrance was marked 1883. So, it made sense that stone carvers sculpted gargoyle figures at the roofline on the Hotel Allen. I never saw them since when I lived in The Allen the gargoyles had deteriorated into weathered stone with no distinguishing features.

Maria poked her head into Estrella's creative space.

"We have a roommate meeting in about an hour. Will that work for you?"

"Yes."

"I'll text you when we are all in the loft and ready to rumble."

Estrella smiled. She wanted to deal with the rent issue and Brad. The infuriation had died by now. She was more curious than angry. She wanted to know what in the world Brad was thinking.

Tired, Estrella lay down for a short nap. Often after painting she felt a kind of call to nap. The batteries needed recharging. Usually this meant a cat nap of not more than ten to twenty minutes. She rarely recalled dreams after napping. She wondered why and often attempted to recall with more focus than after waking up from a nighttime sleep.

Today was different. She experienced a lucid dream, a dream where you are awake in the dream. All the senses are highly acute including inner senses like intuition, telepathy, creative imagination and precognition.

Estrella moved through space at greater and greater speeds until breaking the light barrier. She landed on a distance planet in a star system on the other side of the Milky Way galaxy. She was in a rocket ship but not in a rocket ship at the same time. The thought came to her, 'remember Hofstra.'

Outside, she looked around. There was hustle and bustle. The beings moved about in the air propelled by their thoughts. It was no big deal. It was just how things were on this planet. Estrella moved through the air. She felt proud of herself for her flying skills. The beings there gave supposed prowess no mind. That was the way it was. No big deal.

Episode 27

The text notification pinged. Estrella didn't need to look at it. She knew it was Maria letting her know it was time for the roommate meeting. Maria, Ellen and Sylvia sat waiting for Brad. The tension felt like a ton of bricks. No one felt like chit chat. Friendly smiles and hellos were buried deep inside. Estrella sat down.

Brad made a grand entrance. No one said a word. Silence. Maria, Ellen and Sylvia emanated scorn. They knew Brad much longer and had witnessed and felt his chauvinism many times. Brad plopped down opposite the four creative amigas.

It would have been thoughtful for Brad to break the silence. Since he said nothing, it was apparent, he had no regrets about what he did.

Maria felt it was her place to speak first acting as a ringleader.

"Estrella let us know that she will be moving out next week. She thoughtfully assured us that she will continue to pay rent until we find another roommate. Does anyone have anything to say?"

Silence. All waited for Brad's response. Awkward. Really, everyone wanted to know what Brad was thinking by removing Estrella's paintings from the showing.

"It must be nice to have rich parents," Brad jabbed at Estrella.

Maria, Ellen and Sylvia had gotten to know Estrella. They knew she worked as a server in her parent's café in Segovia. It took more than ten years of hard labor to save for NYC. Brad never made any effort to get to know Estrella. He snap judged her. To him she was a rich girl from Spain.

"My parents are not rich. You work as a waiter, right?"

"Yeah. What's that have to do with anything?"

"I worked as a server in my parent's small café for ten years to save up to move to New York City."

"Displaying gargoyles threated my income. I make my rent for a year from the painting sales at the holiday showing."

"The damage has been done," piped in Maria. The bottom line is Estrella is moving out next week. She wants out of her rent agreement."

"Why? We can't afford to make up the difference," barked Brad.

"Let me finish," responded Maria with needle sharpness. "She has told us she will pay rent until we find someone. She wants to know we will make every effort to find another renter as soon as possible." Ellen and Sylvia nod in agreement.

"I want to be assured that you won't vote against a qualified renter."

"The three of us have decided that if you vote against a qualified renter our three votes will override your one vote," chimed Ellen.

"And, if you persist, we will vote you out as a roommate," warned Sylvia.

"We don't know what your problem is with Estrella. She hasn't done anything to you. You haven't given her the time of day since she moved it," underscored Maria.

"Her art threatens us as working artists. Gargoyles? We don't need Gothic images in the twenty-first century," rebuts Brad.

"Let's not get into a debate about what's art. The bottom line is Estrella cannot create here with your bullshit. Estrella, we wish you the best. We support you. Ellen, Sylvia and I will make every effort to find a replacement roommate as soon as possible."

Episode 28

Estrella moved into Hotel Allen with nothing except her art supplies. She heard about a warehouse for artists in Brooklyn. There were chairs, couches, kitchenware, tables, beds ... most anything needed to furnish an artist's loft. The best thing about the warehouse for artists was everything was free. The second-best thing about the warehouse for artists was they had a truck. Delivery was free, all volunteers. All she needed to buy was bedding – sheets, blankets, pillows. She shopped Macy's Herald Square for those necessities.

Located on the same floor were the offices of Upbeat, the music video company that Luna worked for as their director of social media. They owned the top floor. Besides the Upbeat offices were two apartments. Luna lived down the hall.

Estrella realized she could use Luna's help on social media.

When she studied art in Madrid it was acceptable to visit the art galleries without an appointment and show your portfolio. If the gallery director was busy, then you made an appointment to come back. Galleries in NYC operated differently. Stopping by was taboo. It worked against you. You needed a website, an Instagram, a Facebook, a Twitter and a TikTok. In fact, some artist had their own app.

Estrella hired a website designer through Fivver. It was up and running, estrellapaints.com. She wanted estrellapaintsgargoyles.com but her web designer talked her out of it. The designer argued that she may not always and only paint gargoyles.

Estrella knew she needed to have Luna review her website before she started emailing galleries. In the meantime, she began posting on Instagram. Her handle was estrellapaintsgargolyes. Beside uploading photos of her painting, she posted photos of Hotel Allen and her loft. Otherwise, her days flowed with creativity. Having her own silent space resonated with heaven.

FaceTime. Estrella connected.

"I was just thinking of you."

"Yeah, I was just thinking of me too. That's all I do is think of me," quipped Señor.

"American humor?"

"I don't think I'd call it American. I'd call it dumb humor."

"Como esta mi amiga?"

"Muy bien y tu?"

"Muy, Muy, Muy bien."

"Tres muys. Excelente."

"It's difficult to joke in a non-native language," confessed Estrella. "In Spanish it's easy to joke around. In English, I'm not sure if I'm making any sense."

"We will work on it. How's your new place? Did you find a coffee place for your morning cortado?"

"No, still trying to find a good one. I need to get Miguel to leave Blue Sunrise and become a Village barista."

"Sounds like a plan."

"Señor, have you looked at my website?"

"No. I'll look now. Where do I find it?"

"estrellapaints.com."

"Okay, got it. I don't know much about website design. My publisher takes care of mine."

Episode 29

Over the next three months Estrella emailed most every gallery in Manhattan providing a link to her website, for sure every gallery in the Village. She attended every gallery opening she could find on the internet with the goal of targeting the gallery director with an Instagram, a Facebook post, an email, anything that might get attention. There were no likes, follows or inquiries.

Then one morning on the way to her new favorite coffee shop on University Place she saw a sign in the window of a Hole in the Wall Gallery. It read: "OPEN CALL – TEN ARTISTS TWO PIECES – Submission dates: April 15 – May 14, Opening Reception: Friday, June 2. She took a photo of the sign noting that she needed to follow the submission process through the gallery website: villageart.com.

Estrella geared up. She had more than twenty-five paintings ready to show, ready to sell. She needed to sell soon since she was paying double rent for three months already. The hundred-thousand-euro nest egg was dwindling rapidly. Thoughts crept and popped into her mind about having to get a day job.

Before she completed the showing application, she decided to ask Luna for help on improving her social media and website. Despite living and working on the same floor of the Allen Hotel, they rarely saw each other. Luna traveled a lot promoting Upbeat musical clients.

Besides, Estrella felt uncomfortable around Luna because of her constant social media frenzy.

Estrella walked down to the Upbeat offices for the first time.

"Is Luna in?" asked Estrella of the receptionist.

"No, she's in LA," answered the receptionist matter-of-factly. "Can I give her a message?"

Before Estrella could answer Luna shot into the office with her smartphone drawn. Their eyes met briefly. She was FaceTiming with a client.

"Got to go sweetie. My cousin is here. I'll post those promotional photos on Instagram. What's up neighbor? We live on the same floor, and we never hang out. Let's get a photo together for the Upbeat website. My boss has been asking me to post one of us on our website for weeks."

Before Estrella could respond Luna maneuvered both in front of the reception area giant mirror. Estrella cringed. Mirror selfies made her uncomfortable.

"Relax cousin; smile." Luna snapped off five or six shots. "Estrella you are so pretty, a stunner. You must have men hitting on you all the time."

"I want to ask you about my website. I'm getting no response from the galleries."

"I'll take a look," Luna agreed but it sounded like it would be in the future.

"Luna, I need you to stop a minute and take a look for five minutes. I really need a professional's opinion."

"Hold my calls," commanded Luna.

Estrella followed Luna like a baby duck to its mother. They entered Luna's office. It was twice the size of her apartment office and decorated much like her apartment with bright colors. One entire wall was mirrored. Surprisingly, one of Estrella's paintings hung on the wall."

"You were the one who bought one of my paintings.

"I saw the story about your paintings being stolen from the gallery. I called the gallery and bought one."

"Sight unseen? It's the only painting I've sold so far. I thought the gallery bought it out of guilt."

Episode 30

Luna accessed Estrella's website. She focused with a remarkable concentration. A concentration that Estrella believed Luna did not have. Luna searched the site clicking quickly through the sections. Estrella did not wait patiently. Luna's silence and rapid scanning made her feel uncomfortable.

"At first glance it looks professional, but it doesn't have the "IT" factor. It doesn't pop or keep my attention. First off, it has too many words. You're a painter, a visual artist. Your most visually appealing paintings need to be dominant. Gargoyles are not the most endearing images. Mothers are not going to hang them over their baby's crib."

"So, what do I need to do?" asked Estrella anxiously.

"I'll sit down with our web designer and come up with a more visual, attention getting design."

"My savings are going fast. What is it going to cost?"

"Nothing."

"Why?"

"Upbeat was able to purchase the top floor contingent on assisting at least one Village artist."

"That's great."

"The Village used to be a haven for creative New Yorkers. Most have moved out looking for lower rents."

"Yeah, that's why I rented in Brooklyn. I'm paying double rent until my old roommates find a new artist renter."

"I'll have our web designer do a redesign. We'll have it in a week. I need a selfie bomb for the website. Do it today."

Estrella nodded. She was thankful yet apprehensive. To her, Luna seemed unpredictable and undependable. Luna paid a thousand dollars for the only painting she sold so far. Now she needed to sell dozens more. Being a self-supporting artist was her dream, especially in NYC.

Estrella completed her application to the Hole-In-the-Wall Village art gallery. She waited to send. She wanted to have the new website link to give her the best chance. Only ten artists would be in the show allowing space to display two pieces of art each. Estrella speculated at two thousand each she could make two thousand. The gallery gets fifty percent.

So far living at the Hotel Allen Estrella was obsessed with painting. On the other hand, she did not know anyone in the building. The tenants earned lots of money. They dressed in the finest clothes. When they moved, she noticed the furniture, new and expensive.

Occasionally, someone would say hi or smile. Estrella would nod and smile back. As a server for more than ten years in Segovia her people skills were well honed. Most everyone who works with the public craves alone time. It's the endless people parade. You need to always put on a positive face and use a friendly voice. It eventually burns the social wax in the people candle.

Señor's new book lay unopened on the kitchen counter. Estrella knew he would ask what she thought. He told her the title numerous times, but she couldn't remember. She opened the padded envelop. She read the title: *Mythological Themes in Tattoos*. It sounded fascinating. It seemed like everyone had at least one tattoo. Estrella had thought about getting a gargoyle tattoo but did not trust a tattoo artist with the gargoyle look she would want.

Episode 31

Living in Hotel Allen on the seventh floor required using the elevator. The staircase was an option hidden behind an ominous doorway that looked like a broom closet. Hotel Allen was not a walkup. The state-of-the-art elevator raced to the seventh floor with grace.

Estrella kept a low profile while riding the elevator. A few attempted to make elevator small talk about the weather, the neighborhood or the doorman. She preferred riding up with more than one. It was less awkward than herself and one other. There was a kind of obligation to respond to the other. If they smiled, you felt obligated to return the smile. If they commented on the weather, you felt obligated to respond with a polite nod and 'yeah, it's a beautiful day.'

For Estrella, the most awkward one on one elevator ride was with a handsome young man. Usually, they would cast a flirt or show a hint of charm. If they were first in the elevator, they often would stand by the floor buttons and say, 'what floor?' Estrella usually did not respond but pushed seven just as they completed their offer. If they attempted to engage in a brief elevator dialog, Estrella used a shy smile to deflect any response.

From time to time, she rode the elevator with a well-groomed, well-dressed young man who emanated male model. He would exude superficial charm. Estrella gave him credit for his persistence. No matter what tactic he tried Estrella politely smiled and did not respond. He got off on the sixth floor which gave him time to try whatever he could to make a connection.

Estrella knew he was used to getting his way with women. Most women melted from his fiery charm. Working for a decade at the Aqueduct Café in Segovia, Estrella experienced an international array of male magic.

Living alone was joyful, highly creative, and even spiritual. Lonely? No! She did not need a man to be happy. In middle school she gave her power to crazy love. In fact, to use the word love with crazy meant it really lacked love energy. Obsession with another led to a possessiveness, led to relationship drama and a breakup.

The rollercoaster emotion of crazy love scared her deeply. Being madly in love and head over heels lost its compulsion by the time she went to high school. Because of her stunning beauty boys literally lined up to try their hand at being her boyfriend. Falling in love was exactly that, falling. What happens when you fall down? Injury, broken bones, scrapes, scratches and bruises follow.

Estrella shared one story of first love. Hopelessly in love with Marcos in eighth grade, Estrella thought day and especially at night about him. They attended the same Catholic schools since kindergarten. He was her first kiss. One day they met secretly after school. Holding hands, they walked up to the Alcazar Castle where King Ferdinand and Queen Isabella lived during Medieval times. Walt Disney modeled the Fantasyland castle after Alcazar.

Marco's cousin managed the ticket office. He let them enter for free. They knew the castle backwards and forwards. Off limit rooms and alcoves suited their need for privacy. Marcos's kisses felt like sunlight and wind. How was it possible to feel so alive? Nothing else mattered. Food, water, family and school had no attraction.

One day the museum director happened to enter one of their favorite rooms. The scandal rocked Segovia. Marcos was expelled. His parents sent him to Madrid to live with his uncle. Estrella's parents grounded her for months. That's when she discovered painting.

Episode 32

First thing every morning Estrella checked her email to see if the Hole in the Wall Gallery selected her for the opening. So far, no such luck. The deadline loomed. This morning the only email she received was from her mother. Her mom and dad were coming to NYC to visit at the same time as the gallery opening.

This threw her into a tailspin. Her parents thought she painted pretty flowers. Her dad, Roberto, especially thought becoming an artist was not worth Estrella's time. He wanted to retire in the next couple of years and hoped Estrella would take over the café. He also hoped she would settle down, get married and have children.

Her mom, Rosa, was traditional too but supported Estrella in whatever she wanted to do even if she thought it wasn't the best. Being a

Catholic girl motherhood was expected despite any personal dreams or goals. Rosa dreamed of being a scientist, a biologist. University wasn't an option. Motherhood was the only option. She wanted Estrella to follow her dreams.

Estrella wondered where they would stay. She worried about inviting them to the gallery opening or not. She thought maybe they would be more supportive if they attended the opening and saw her paintings being sold. On the other hand, she thought about how they would feel about her gargoyles. More than likely they would not approve.

Estrella got dressed and headed to her new, favorite Handcraft Coffee two doors down from Hole in the Wall Gallery. Her mind raced to the point that she felt out of control. Passing the gallery, she noticed the Call for Artists sign was no longer in the window.

While sipping a cortado Estrella scratched out some numbers on a napkin. She needed to know where she stood. Paying double rent, several thousand a month, was draining her bank account. She didn't want to work a day job confining her painting to her days off. She did that for years in Segovia.

She decided to call Maria and find out what was happening. She finished her cortado, left Hand Craft Coffee and walked the short distance to Washington Square Park. She found a bench, sat and called Maria.

"Hello, hi Estrella. Sorry I didn't respond to your texts," apologized Maria.

"Hi Maria. Any luck on finding another roommate to take over my rent?"

"I just got back from Cleveland from visiting my parents."

"Oh, how are they doing? My parents are coming here to visit."

"Sadly, my dad has prostate cancer. They are trying to figure out how bad it is."

"So sorry Maria."

"I'm worried. Fortunately, he's not in any pain right now. I'm so sorry we have not found a roommate yet. Artists are leaving the city for places in upstate New York and cities like Cleveland, Pittsburgh and Minneapolis. An artist needs to be making really big money to afford living in our loft."

"When does the loft lease come up for renewal?"

"This summer. Ellen, Sylvia and I are thinking about not renewing. I may go back to Cleveland. Ellen and Sylvia may be looking for another place. After what happened with Brad there's a lot of tension in the loft."

"I love Hotel Allen, but the double rent is killing me. If I don't get an opening and sell some paintings, I'm looking at going back to work."

Episode 33

As soon as Estrella got back to her Hotel Allen loft, she checked her email hoping to see something from the Hole in the Wall Gallery. Nothing. She was tempted to go down to the gallery and ask in person. The Call for Artists clearly stated not to go to the gallery and make inquiries. Between the finances, madre and padre visiting and waiting for the gallery showing worry consumed Estrella.

She knew the only thing that could get her out of her worry pit was to paint. Painting got her out of her head. Creating was a natural high. Time flew by. Colors came alive with a natural neon glow.

The day evaporated into dusk. She put down her brush and sat facing the western sky window. The building across University Place partially blocked a full view sunset. Still, there was a sliver of the sunset spectrum of oranges, pinks and purples. Painting aligned her with the universal presence transforming worry and fear into joy and bliss.

The sunset transformed into night. There was too much light pollution and smog to see any stars. Still, the crescent moon lined up perfectly in the sliver between buildings across University Place. A song Estrella's mom sang came to mind. It played in her mind.

I travel near, I travel far,

I do not rise like any star,

While comets like to run a race,

A star rises in the same place,

Please try to remember what I say,

Stars rise and set in a regular way.

The iPhone FaceTimed. Señor's face shined. Estrella could always tell when another creative person had been savoring muse energy.

"Hi Señor."

"I just finished painting for today."

"You sound stoned."

"High on creative energy. You know I'm not a stoner."

"Yeah, I know. You might want to loosen up once in a while. What's going on? Any word on the artist selection?"

"Nothing, you're coming to the opening, right?"

"Do you need to ask?"

"What's happening in Bar Harbor?"

"I'm gazing out the window at a billion-star night sky with *Twinkle, Twinkle Little Star* playing in my head."

"I know you're going to ask me if I read your tattoo book yet."

"Did you read my tattoo book?"

"No, not yet."

"Don't feel guilty or anything."

"Stop teasing. You know I have Catholic guilt."

"I'm coming to the city for a book signing at Barnes & Noble on Fifth Avenue. You got to be there. I want to introduce you to a couple who live on Billionaire's Row. They're on the board at the Guggenheim. Maybe they can get you into one of the showings. Plus, I just want you there."

"When is it?"

"Saturday, June 3."

"Perfect, you can go to my opening on June 2."

Episode 34

Señor drove down from Bar Harbor for Estrella's opening and his book signing. He parked for free at his publisher's garage uptown and took the subway to 14th street. He walked to 10th Street and entered the hotel. He heard a lot about Hotel Allen from creative people who lived in the hotel before the renovation. In the old days creative people could afford the cheap rent.

He knocked on the Estrella's door. The door sprung open almost instantly to Señor's surprise.

"How'd you know I was here?"

"You are always on time. I didn't get picked for the Hole in the Wall Gallery opening tonight."

Señor ignored Estrella's snappy confession.

"Wow! This place must cost you a fortune. Give me the tour."

"Yeah, it's draining my savings. But it's worth it. I'm painting every day and loving it. This way." Estrella guided Señor toward the back where a massive amount of light filled the painting studio.

Señor immediately noticed finished paintings leaning against the wall. There had to be at least twenty-five.

"You're not kidding about painting every day. I'm sorry you didn't get chosen for the opening tonight. I say we go anyway. You said it was just down the street."

"No, we can't. My parents are flying into town, and I lied to them saying the gallery opening was postponed."

"I thought you said they are arriving about 9. What time is the opening?"

"Seven."

"Let's go right at seven and head to the airport at 7:30. You need to toughen up. This is NYC. We can take a cab uptown to my car and pick up your parents. By the way, where are they staying? I'm sure not at your loft."

"Okay, let's do the opening. I got them reservations at Washington Square Hotel. They are going to be jet lag tired. I will be like three am Spain time."

I knew Estrella needed to loosen up, go more with the flow, not be so serious about her painting. I learned as a writer that if I wanted it too much and spent all my spare time on writing and not enjoying other things in life that in a way, I was pushing success away.

Billy pointed this out. When he first mentioned it, I got defensive. I was raised with the belief that if you wanted something you needed to work hard for it. Billy told me there are different kinds of working hard. Working too hard is not mentally healthy. Working smart and just enough is wiser and leads to a more fruitful success.

I began to explore other hobbies from taking long walks and bike rides in Central Park to enjoying days off with friends without talking or thinking about writing. I began to play guitar again for fun.

Almost immediately I noticed a more relaxed, fluid writing style. Rather than push and force the writing, the writing flowed without struggle. I stopped forcing myself to always have a writing schedule. Yes, I need the discipline, but I no longer always had to write from eight to noon. Sometimes I noticed I needed not to force it. Sometimes I'd take a walk then come back and write.

Episode 35

We arrived at the Hole in the Wall Gallery exactly at 7:30. We both felt uncomfortable being the first. The gallery owner introduced herself.

"Welcome. Thanks for coming. I'm Betty, the gallery owner." She graciously extended her hand. We both shook her hand.

"Hi Betty. My friends call me Señor. At least that's what Estrella calls me. Estrella is a painter living at the Hotel Allen."

"Hi Betty," Estrella said awkwardly."

"What's your medium," Betty inquired.

"Painting."

"You need to respond to our next Call for Artist."

"Estrella responded to this show but wasn't selected," piped Señor. Estrella felt horrified. "Oh, what's your name?"

"Estrella."

"Oh, yes, I remember your paintings, gargoyles. I seriously considered showing your work tonight but saw you were a Spanish citizen. I had a bad experience selling art from a foreign artist." Estrella was taken aback.

"She has a work permit. I helped her get it," Señor assured Betty.

"I love your work Estrella. Bring me a copy of your work permit and let's have you show in the fall."

"Okay." Estrella felt an ecstatic rush.

"Please excuse me. I need to get the cheese, crackers and wine prepped. Look around," invited Betty.

Estrella scanned the walls. Her eyes locked on large, bright colored flowers on three feet by three-foot canvases. Brad. Brad made the show. Estrella darted her eyes front to back and side to side searching for Brad.

"We've got to go," insisted Estrella.

"We just got here," responded Señor.

"Seriously, we need to go and now," demanded Estrella.

Just then Brad entered the gallery. He didn't notice Estrella. He beelined toward the back of the gallery probably to check in with Betty.

"Who is he? You look like you have seen one of your gargoyles."

"He's my ex-roommate who took my paintings from my show in Brooklyn. He's the reason I moved from the Brooklyn loft to Hotel Allen. I can't believe he's in this show."

"You never really found out why he removed your art from the show."

"He just didn't like my work. He said it was too Gothic not modern."

"You need to ask him right here and now. Go back there and say hello and ask him without attacking him."

"Seriously Señor, we need to go."

"No, you need to deal with this now. It's no accident we are here early. You're a big girl now and making it in the Big Apple."

Estrella knew Señor was right. If she would have had it out with Brad back in the Brooklyn loft maybe she could have stayed instead of moving out on impulse and paying for two huge rents.

Episode 36

I saw Estrella disappear into the back of the gallery. I walked around viewing the art while several other gallery patrons entered. There were ten to fifteen of us now. The next ten minutes seemed like twenty. It felt like Estrella let Brad know in no uncertain term.

Part of me could not wait to find out what was said, discussed and emoted. Finally, Estrella walked confidently from the back of the gallery toward to where I was standing. She appeared relieved.

"Let's go," Estrella commanded. I hesitated but deferred to her wishes.

"Yeah, let's go. We are going." Estrella led the way out of the gallery. She had no interest in seeing the art. She was all business. She hailed a taxi with a strong raised hand.

I told the driver the address for my publisher's parking garage uptown. We did not speak. I wanted to ask Estrella what was said. I could feel she wasn't going to tell me if I asked so I resisted. I knew she could feel my gripping curiosity. We both just let it go. Once we got into my car, I felt it was okay to speak as long as I did not ask about Brad.

"JFK, right?"

"Yeah, the same terminal I arrived at." Estrella searched the American Airlines app.

"It's on time, 8:55."

I hadn't met Estrella's parents. So, I felt a bit uncomfortable. Estrella hadn't shared anything about our friendship with her parents. I decided to just go with the flow and take Estrella's lead. I wondered if they would be hungry. Did we need to take them out to dinner? I asked to myself.

"I told my mother you were a writer friend who had a car. I knew she would pass that along to papa softening the information as matter of fact."

We pulled up to the terminal entrance. I dropped off Estrella. She said she would text me when they finished Customs and baggage claim. I drove out of JFK and found a free place to park. I listened to jazz on Sirius XM radio. I decided to keep my mouth shut other than to formal greetings.

I really looked forward to the book signing of *Mythological Themes in Tattoos*. I spent two years taking photographs of my friends' tattoos. One of my favorites was what I called the Minaret Temple Tattoo. The tattoo is located on the upper inside of the left arm between the elbow and the bicep. The left side is often associated with the feminine goddess energy. My nickname for Gabrielle was Goddess.

Goddess told me her original idea was that an image would invoke the feeling of a "queen and her castle." Before meeting with the tattoo artist, she found a photo of a mosque with four spiraling minarets surrounding it. This image provided a starting point for the tattoo artist. At that appointment the two then collaborated on refining the idea.

As they discussed the tattoo, a song played, the Gothic rock classic *Temple of Love* by the English band Sisters of Mercy. The castle tattooed by the artist evolved into the Minaret Temple

Tattoo. I decided to recommend Estrella use the song when she has a major opening. Afterall, the Holy Cathedral of Segovia inspired her gargoyle paintings. It is one of the largest Medieval Catholic churches in Spain. It's devoted to the Assumption of the Virgin Mary, the Catholic goddess.

Estrella's text came. I headed for the terminal entrance. Despite Estrella and her parents speaking in Spanish. I decided to tell this story in English. JFK wasn't too busy for a Friday night. It only took ten minutes to pull up to the customs terminal.

Episode 37

I hopped out of the car, opened the trunk, and saw Estrella conversing mostly with her mother. Taking up the rear, Estrella's father managed two large suitcases. He stumbled and bumbled in a slapstick kind of way. I wanted to laugh but kept it to a smile. I waved. Estrella saw me.

I felt like an Uber driver heading back to The Village and Washington Square Hotel. Estrella and her mom spoke Spanish at the speed of sound in the back seat. Her dad sat in the front seat and said nothing. I could tell he felt awkward, self-conscious. He knew I spoke Spanish and studied in Madrid. We didn't even talk about the weather. The half hour drive seemed like two hours.

I dropped them off at their hotel and headed for Billy's place in Brooklyn. Estrella got them checked in and settled in their room. They were agonizingly tired. Afterall, it was after three am Segovia time. Estrella walked back to Hotel Allen.

Parked in the yellow zone at the front entrance was Brad. They briefly greeted each other. Brad opened the back of the van revealing about ten large paintings. They carried them to the freight elevator and brought them up to Estrella's artist loft.

It felt like a clandestine mission. Estrella struck a deal with Brad. He agreed to bring his paintings over so that Estrella could pass them off as hers. Estrella didn't want her parents to see the gargoyles. Her father especially would not approve. Not only did Brad help with his paintings he assisted Estrella in covering all her paintings with old sheets. Brad's large, colorful flowers paintings took center stage.

Estrella was up early. Instead of going to Hand Craft Coffee for her morning cortado she waited for her mother's text. She planned to meet up with her parents, go for coffee and then bring them to her Hotel Allen loft to see her paintings.

Anxious, Estrella paced around the loft looking for any lapse in hiding gargoyles.

The text finally appeared. Estrella strolled toward Washington Square Park. She was at once free and in the moment and repressed in the past restricted by Segovia religious, family belief systems.

There was no need to go up to the room. Her parents were waiting in the lobby. Her father seemed to be out of place, a fish out of water. At Aqueduct Café he was the king in his castle, the big fish in the pond. It was clear to Estrella that her mother talked papa into coming.

On the way to Hotel Allen, they stopped at Hand Craft Coffee for cortados. Papa took a sip and hilariously wanted to spit it out. He was too much of Catholic to spit so he swallowed his pride.

"They clearly do not know how to make a cortado," he blared authoritatively. "The milk tastes like water."

"They use low fat milk here," Estrella shared matter-of-factly.

"That's not milk; the fat makes the milk. It gives it flavor, especially in a cortado."

Papa left the cortado. Estrella loved the Hand Craft cortado with low-fat or soymilk. Mama loved trying new things both in food and culture. Estrella was more like her mom that way. She was more like her dad when it came to pride in work. Papa patiently fidgeted. He emanated the feeling of being perpetually out of place. He didn't fit it. The customers kept glancing and staring at him. They smiled at his awkward vibe. Papa wanted to be home.

Estrella and mama chit chatted about the planned day's events. Mama wanted to be sure to visit with Luna. Luna's mother was mama's sister. Apparently, Luna's mother rarely heard from her adventurous daughter. Instagram and Tik-Tok were the social media that allowed for a semblance of connection.

Episode 38

Walking back to the Hotel Allen Estrella made every effort to chit chat with papa. Even though she and mama had more in common she felt a kind of mysterious, deep soul connection with papa. Talking with him was always awkward. He clearly was not a talker. He was a doer.

He bought the Aqueduct Café in 1969. He borrowed the money from his papa and paid every centavo back. They worked long hours, 5 am to midnight, seven days a week. Locals loved the café especially since mama was the greeter. She loved to know how everyone was doing. Tourists loved the café because it was convenient, and mama made everyone feel welcome.

Estrella struggled to get the conversation going. Questions about the flight from Spain, who was running the café while they were gone, did he plan on retiring or selling the café and more flickered through her mind. Estrella wanted to go deeper. What would touch his soul? What would ignite his genuine interest?

Papa loved to fish in the Eresma River. In the winter, when there were fewer tourists, papa would close the café during siesta. Instead of napping he would head to the river to fish. When I was six, he would stop by my school once a month and pick me up. He took me fishing.

Papa was old school. He wanted a son. He was steeped in European patriarchy. They tried for another child. It just didn't happen. I was the tom boy replacement.

I loved the silence, the river, the fishing and doing something outside the café with papa. We didn't catch many brown trout. We didn't talk much. I felt papa's love, stability and security. It gave me confidence.

Sometimes we caught enough trout that we added it to the café menu. Papa was a master cook. When brown trout went on the menu the word of mouth was faster than the internet. The locals flocked to the café.

We made it back to Hotel Allen. I never said a word to papa. I wanted to strike up a conversation about fishing the Eresma River. I wished they were staying in New York longer. I heard trout fishing in upstate New York in the Catskill Mountains was the best.

"Here we are." I attempted to break the ice. Papa nodded his head slightly. Mama kept quiet during the five-minute walk from Hand Craft Coffee. She wanted us to renew our bond. Papa was vehemently against the move to New York. A daughter needed to marry and have children. Patriarchy reigns in many parts of the world.

We exited the elevator. Estrella led her parents down the hall to her loft apartment. As they entered, she focused on mama's face looking for her approval.

"You have so much space. This is bigger than our apartment on the aqueduct plaza. And the light. It's bright." Mama loved it. Papa's face remained stoic.

"Thank you, mama. I love it too. It's my dream space."

"Let's see your paintings. I've never seen any of your work. We couldn't make it to your Madrid art openings. We needed to run the café."

Estrella guided her parents to studio central. The large flower paintings in vibrant colors dominated. Papa's eyes lit up. He didn't say anything, but he didn't need to. He liked them. Mama smiled. She loved them.

Episode 39

"Doesn't Luna live here too? Mama asked matter-of-factly.

"Yes, she lives and works on this floor. She's on her way to say hi."

Just then there was a knock at the door. Estrella opened the door. Luna paraded in to greet her aunt and uncle.

"Welcome to New York City," Luna spoke with positivity.

Mama gave Luna a warm hug. "Are you coming to the book signing tonight."

"I didn't not know there was a book signing," Luna glanced with puzzlement at Estrella.

"I didn't think you'd be interested," Estrella defended herself.

"It's open to the public. You're welcome to come." Estrella felt uncomfortable when Luna attended social events. She always had to make a splash.

"What are you wearing Estrella? You need to shine. A Fifth Avenue book signing may lead to a gallery opening. We're about the same size. Come down to my place we'll pick out an outfit."

"Oh, I don't know. My parents are here."

"Estrella, honey, your father and I want to explore. Go ahead. We'll see you later."

"Are you sure?"

"Yes, I'm sure."

Luna led Estrella to her apartment. Estrella had been to Luna's office but never to her apartment. Honestly, Estrella avoided her cousin. She felt uncomfortable with the flamboyant lifestyle.

There were mirrors, bright colored furniture, and framed photographs. Luna shot a video and posted it on Tik-Tok. Luna knew social media and how to wield it.

"My star cousin you live in New York. You're an artist. You must be fashion aware. If you go to openings, signings, social events dressed drably, then you will go unnoticed.

"Do you have HBO MAX?"

"What's that?"

"My star cousin you need to join the twenty-first century. It's a streaming television channel."

"I don't watch television."

"You have an iPhone; you have a MacBook Pro. You can watch on either. You need to get HBO. I'll get you set up with my password. You need to watch *Bill Cunningham New York.* He was the fashion photographer for the New York Times for fifty years. It's a must."

Estrella listened and resisted simultaneously. Fashion wasn't her thing. She recognized Luna's assistance on her website made a difference. Luna opened her closet door like a stage curtain. It was more a room than a closet.

"Let's see. You need color. Yet you need something that says I paint gargoyles. Black and grey. I got it, orange."

"I don't want to look like a pumpkin. Besides, my parents will be with me."

"My star you are not your parents. Tonight, is your coming out party. If you want to be a successful painter in the creative capital of the world you need to dress the part. Here, try this on."

Luna handed Estrella a chic black dress with a plunging neckline, a pair of orange high heels and a bright orange chiffon scarf. She reluctantly changed.

Episode 40

Señor pulled up to Hotel Allen and texted Estrella, 'I'm here.' Estrella texted back, 'I'll be right down.' Billy sat in the front seat. Estrella climbed into the back seat. She got intense looks from both Señor and Billy.

"Don't say anything. I don't want to talk about it."

"Okay," retorted Señor. "So, what did you do with your parents today?"

"Go to Washington Square Park; they are staying at the Washington Square Hotel. We did the tourist stops, Time Square, the Empire State Building and the Statue of Liberty."

"No tour of your art studio?"

"That was the first stop this morning."

"And? What was their reaction to your gargoyle paintings?"

"I'd rather talk about your book signing. When mi madre asked what your book was about, I said it was about mythological themes in tattoos. I felt that was enough for them to handle. Hi Billy."

"I for one think you look great."

"Thanks."

A brief stint of welcomed silence felt good to Señor, Billy and Estrella. They knew the night would be laden with words, some meaningful but mostly meaningless word noises.

Mama and Papa stood at the hotel entrance. Estrella waved when they pulled up. Estrella got out of the car and held the door open for her parents.

"This is Billy, Señor's best friend.

"Welcome to New York City."

"Dressed pretty," observed mama. "Luna has an eye for fashion."

Arriving at Barnes & Noble Fifth Avenue, it was apparent it was a New York City event. Hollywood searchlights spun bright. Classy black suit clad valets parked cars. The front window boasted a giant poster of Señor's book cover featuring his favorite tattoo, the Minaret Temple Tattoo by Goddess Gabrielle.

Exiting the car, papa's eyes revealed awkward discomfort, not even comfortable discomfort. He really didn't want to be there. Entering the bookstore, he noticed a parade of tattooed customers. Estrella didn't warn her parents that the book premier coincided with the New York City Tattoo artists' annual convention.

Señor's publisher greeted him at the door and guided him to the book signing table where there was already a line of about a hundred. Billy stayed with Estrella and her parents taking on a supportive roll.

"We didn't know you had a famous friend," commented mama.

"I think tonight is his first fifteen minutes of fame," responded Estrella.

The publisher's personal assistant guided them to the VIP room. Wine, Champagne, charcuterie and chocolate truffles greeted the special guests. Papa loved chocolate truffles with Rioja Spanish wine. He felt more comfortable.

Copies of *Mythological Themes in Tattoos* were stacked on a shelf. The publisher's personal assistant let everyone know there was a signed copy for all including one for mama and one for papa.

A photographer eased up to Estrella. "May I take some photos? I'm the fashion photographer for the New York Times."

Episode 41

Estrella hesitated. She did not want to use her genetic good looks to promote her painting career.

"Go ahead, Estrella," urged mama.

"I'm William James. Everybody calls me Willy. The Times won't publish anything you don't approve in writing."

"Let him take some photos. You look so pretty tonight."

Estrella nodded a weak okay.

"Continue with your evening. I don't take posed photos. If I see an impromptu moment, I'll take a photo. If the Times wants to publish a photo, I will email you for your permission with a copy of the photo."

Willy moved on, flowing with the people attending the book signing. Just then a couple in their forties stepped up to Estrella. She wasn't used to all the attention.

"Are you Estrella?" asked a woman wearing all designer.

"Yes," replied Estrella with a slight defensiveness.

"We are Betty and Robert Morgan, good friends with Señor. We want you and your parents to join us at the after party at The Players."

"Thank you," interjected mama before Estrella could answer.

"What's The Players," inquired Estrella.

"The Players is a club of artists, art lovers, writers, actors and musicians," clarified Robert.

"Your mother tells us you're a painter," added Betty. "We support the creative arts. Robert and I are on the board at the Guggenheim."

"I love the Guggenheim," Estrella responded.

"Great, Señor will show you to our limousine after the signing."

After two Spanish red wines, vino tintos, papa joined the party. Mama glowed with excitement. Estrella loosened up to the attention.

She felt grateful to Luna for her insistence on looking New York chic.

I finished signing over a hundred books or more. Good thing my publisher brought extra Sharpies. By hand cramped up toward the end. Next, I spoke about the Temple Minaret Tattoo on the cover with Goddess Gabrielle and the tattoo artist.

My elated publisher radiated success. In the nineteen seventies about fifty thousand books were published in the United States. Now, with desk top publishing, self-publishing and digital printing more than a million books a year are published worldwide.

Most of the younger generation rather watch entertaining videos or see amazing images than read hundreds of pages. What do you expect? YouTube, streaming movies in the home, free audio books and endless podcasts compete with books for engaging likes.

After reading and presenting the Temple Minaret Tattoo, we exited onto Fifth Avenue. The Morgan's chauffer greeted us with a smile and a tip of his hat. We all piled in. Myself, my publisher,

Billy, Estrella, mama, papa and the Morgan's. We were off to The Players in Gramercy Park.

The Players is a private social club founded in New York City by the noted 19th-century Shakespearean actor Edwin Booth. In 1888, Booth purchased an 1847 mansion at 16 Gramercy Park, reserved an upper floor for his residence, and turned the rest into a clubhouse.

Past members included artists Jackson Pollock, Andy Warhol and Estrella's favorite, Georgia O'Keefe. Some of the famous actors include Jimmy Fallon, Cary Grant, Tommy Lee Jones and Emma Watson.

Episode 42

The Players felt exclusive because it was. Chill music played. Photos of famous Player's members past and present adorned the white walls in the main corridor. Betty Morgan and mama chattered. Robert Morgan, I, Billy and Estrella formed a group. Papa navigated his own world.

Billy and Robert got caught up in a conversation. Estrella and I verbally riffed.

"Does Billy have a girlfriend?" Estrella asked.

"No, why?" I responded.

"I don't know. I just wondered."

"He's a good man, solid. But he's not exactly a handsome man. Women aren't attracted to him. He's a cross between the hunchback of Notre Dame, the Beast and Cyrano de Bergerac."

"He's not that ugly," defended Estrella.

"What's going on in your love life?" asked Señor.

"Nothing. I'm not interested. Relationships take up too much time and energy. I moved to New York to be a painter not a girlfriend."

"Since you asked me, I'm asking you. Do you have a woman friend in Bar Harbor?"

"No, I'm all in on creativity. My life is writing. Relationships often take up too much time and energy, especially if there's drama."

"Don't you miss being close with someone?"

"I love my friends. They are my family. Between you and me I see a professional cuddle-hugger."

"What's that?"

"They cuddle and hug platonically."

"And you pay them?"

"Yes. For me, it's a healing. It's a kind, communicative exchange for an hour. There's no drama or negative, romantic love possessiveness."

"Wow! Are men professional huggers?"

"I don't know. You can check it out on the cuddle-hugger.com website."

The conversation was cut short when the female DJ duo TESSLA spun a record. The party got started. Dancing, disco ball and dim lighting transformed The Player into a nightclub. The strobe lights electrified the myriad of tattoos.

Mama signaled Estrella to step outside. The air was thick with New York City night. A Saturday night crescendo of upbeat energy welcomed conversation.

"Guess what?" Asked mama.

"I'm not guessing. Just tell me."

"We are flying back to Spain in the Morgan's private 767 jet. They're dropping us off in Madrid and then they are off to Paris."

"You guys must have really hit it off."

"They live on billionaires' row on Fifty-Seventh Street. They own an entire skyscraper floor. She wants to commission a painting. You need to talk with her tonight. She wants to see your website and Instagram. Show her on your phone, tonight."

"That's amazing."

Episode 43

By midnight The Player party came to an end. The lights came up and the revelers headed for the doors. Robert Morgan passed the word that he was paying for Ubers for all who wanted to go to The Box nightclub. We climbed into the Morgan limo and headed home.

Estrella wanted to discuss the commission with Betty but didn't want her parents to hear about her gargoyles. She did manage to get Betty's email address so they could stay in touch. Billy and I got dropped off at my car parked at Barnes & Noble Fifth Avenue. Mama and Papa got dropped off at Washington Square Hotel and Estrella at Hotel Allen.

During the next month Estrella emailed Betty several times but received no response. She needed the money. She called Maria to see if they had rented her loft space to another artist. No such luck. Artists were leaving the city for locations with affordable rents. The good news was the Brooklyn loft lease ended in August.

Estrella knew her parents could afford to help her out financially. But Papa did not approve of her move to New York City to pursue a painting career. The next Hole in the Wall Gallery opening wasn't until after Labor Day weekend. Estrella might be able to make some sales then. In the meantime, she needed to find a job to make her savings last.

The baristas at Hand Craft Coffee mentioned numerous times that Hand Craft was opening another store in The Cellar in Macy's Herald Square. She applied for a barista position. With more than a decade of experience and a working visa she easily got the job. Speaking Spanish worked in her favor too. At the Aqueduct Cafe she served customers from around the world. The Cellar served customers from most every country. Working full time reduced her painting time to her days off, Mondays and Tuesdays.

Estrella felt the working grind of NYC. The alarm clock, the rush to get ready, the ride on the subway, the city noises, the hustle and bustle, the clock punch, the morning line for coffee: Estrella began feeling like a New Yorker not a Spaniard from Segovia.

Over the years Estrella noticed how many classmates, friends, family members and acquaintances expressed and enjoyed creative expression but succumbed to the demands of so called modern, capitalist life. She needed creative energy as much as food, water and air. Whenever she got away from painting for too long her health suffered.

She was determined to keep your creative energies flowing. During her hour lunch break she sketched and made notes. This always gave a kind of inner nourishment. Often her co-workers wanted to talk about random hum drum. She resisted politely. Some thought she was a snob. Others saw her as aloof. Still others pegged her as an introvert.

What she earned as a barista paid for food and power. She didn't earn enough to pay all the rents. The financial stress sometimes got to her. Not making it and moving back to Segovia filled her with dread. That feeling froze her soul and cut off her creativity.

Estrella endeared her customers. Many returned day after day wanting her to make their cortado. She was missed on Mondays and Tuesdays. The Spanish mission to the United Nations was located on forty-seventh street.

When word got out that Estrella made the best cortado in Manhattan, the employees stopped for a cortado to go and walked the mile from thirty-fourth street. By August the Spanish mission counted Estrella as an honorary employee. Many of the workers were from Madrid where Estrella attended University. She began to have a following.

Her website got a lot of visits from her Spanish mission customers. They enjoyed ordering in Spanish. Several promised to attend her gallery opening at the Hole in the Wall.

Episode 44

The first month at Macy's Hand Craft Coffee went well. Estrella became the queen of coffee in the Macy's Cellar. However, after the first month things began to unravel. Sara, the assistant manager, resented Estrella. She did not like that Estrella was getting all the attention. Sara had nine years' experience in The Cellar. She rose to assistant manager of the Starbucks before it was replaced by Hand Craft

Sara scheduled Estrella differently from week to week. There were no more two days in a row, Mondays, and Tuesdays. Instead, Sara scheduled Estrella off on Tuesday and Friday. Then she scheduled her off Monday and Wednesday. This made it difficult for Estrella to get into a creative flow. Sara changed her working hours from week to week. One week she had Estrella open at six a.m. The next week she had her start at three p.m.

Sara wanted the spotlight. Whenever Sara worked Estrella was assigned pricing and stocking duties. Whenever shipments arrived Sara had Estrella work receiving in the back. The customers asked if Estrella had left Hand Craft. Those who loved her cortado were out of luck. Sara made their cortados leaving them disappointed.

Estrella hadn't experience sustained cruelty before. Afterall, she worked for papa at the Aqueduct Café. Papa was a task master, but he wasn't mean or dictatorial. Sara was vicious with a smile. No one would suspect Sara singled out Estrella. Things got to a point that Estrella considered leaving Macy's. That's exactly what Sara wanted.

For the rest of the summer Estrella struggled with her painting. She had difficulty getting into a groove. And if she did catch a wave of creative energy, she couldn't sustain it two days in a row. She had to wait at least a week to pick up where she left off. For the first time since moving to NYC she had difficulty finishing paintings.

Estrella and I FaceTimed about her job woes several times a week. I suggested she meet with Sara and share her concerns. Every time Estrella set up meeting Sara cancelled. Then I suggested she go to human resources. That led nowhere and actually made things worse. Sara had been sending emails to HR complaining about Estrella's poor performance and requesting she be moved to another department.

Exasperated, Estrella seriously considered leaving Macy's. I suggested a counter offensive. Estrella contacted the U.N. Spanish Mission customers and asked them to write emails and send letters to HR requesting she make cortados during the busy morning hours. Sara got wind of this, and it flipped her lid.

This meant war. Sara bought out the heavy artillery. Every Macy's employee had a locker. Estrella kept her working shoes in her locker. She learned while working at the Aqueduct Café to wear ultra-comfortable shoes. Standing all day took a toll on the feet and legs. Estrella's locker was broken into, and her shoes stolen. She bought another pair, and her locker was broken into again.

The shoes were stolen. Estrella had no proof, but she knew Sara was behind the thefts.

Estrella asked security to review the locker room footage. Coincidently, only on those days were the locker room security cameras being repaired. I have to say I was running out of ideas. Taking it to the next level meant sinking down to Sara's level. I was making great money from book sales. I thought about hiring a private detective to follow Sara around for a couple of weeks. The private eye could dig into Sara's past behavior with other employees to see if there was a pattern.

Estrella and I are creative people. We don't have time for petty battles. It drains away the precious creative energies. We finally decided to just let it go. Estrella took the Gandhi and MLK approach.

Episode 45

As the job stress went up the painting went down. Estrella had more than ten years serving the public. Just about every situation from positive to negative she had encountered and dealt with. Her boss was papa all those years. Sara was a harassing bitch from the streets of Brooklyn. If she didn't like you then you were on the outs.

We decided Estrella needed to think of the situation differently and stop referring to Sara as a bitch. The doctrine of non-violence is sort of like the Christian turning of the other cheek. When it came right down to it Estrella needed to change how she reacted and thought about the situation. She realized she could not control Sara, but she could choose how she reacted.

Everything came to a head one afternoon. Sara reprimanded how Estrella cleaned up after the morning and midday shifts. Believe me Estrella was a meticulous clearer. Papa obsessed on making everything spotless. Clearly, Sara was busting balls for no reason other than harassment.

"I told you at least a hundred times when you clean the counters to use the cleanser spray first then wipe it down with a dry cloth," squealed Sara.

In the past Estrella would react by defending herself with resentment, anger and you are wrong attitude. This time she sucked it up, let it go, took a deep breath and then responded genuinely.

"Thank you, Sara for pointing out my mistake. I will redo it immediately. When I'm done, I'll have you inspect it to be sure I'm doing exactly how it needs to be done."

Sara was taken aback. It threw her for a loop. She was thrown a curve ball. She didn't know what to do. If she couldn't get to Estrella by attacking, then she felt she had no power over her. She plotted her next attack. A few minutes later she launched another offensive.

"Stop cleaning the counters and clean the coffee grinder. I told you to clean it last week and it still isn't done," Sara barked.

Estrella's first thought was to retaliate defensively by saying, 'you never asked me to clean the bean grinder.' She caught herself and replied. "So sorry, I will get it done immediately. Do you want me to finish the counters after that?" Estrella was getting the hang of register but don't react. She went into neutral which stopped feeding Sara the energy she needed for power.

Estrella kept it up for days. Every time Sara attacked Estrella calmly responded without antagonism. Amazingly, Sara began to leave Estrella alone. Unfortunately, she started to pick on the new barista with relentless assaults. The feeling of liberation Estrella felt inspired her. She felt less tired after work. She began painting in the evening and into the nights. These paintings were some of her best. They would be perfect for the Hole in the Wall Gallery opening.

Estrella came to work one day, and the Hand Craft Coffee Cellar manager announced that Sara had left for another job as the regional manager for Starbucks. After she left everything was different. The United Nations missions from Spain, Central and South America lined up every morning for cortados. Her cortados became NYC famous for the steamed milk gargoyles on top.

Episode 46

Mama skyped Estrella asking why she hadn't contacted Betty Morgan about the commission for their 57th Street high rise overlooking Central Park. Estrella knew she emailed Betty several times. Each time she politely waited the socially accepted time before emailing again. Never a response.

Mama sent an email to Betty and cc'd Estrella. 'Hope all is well in Paris. Estrella has tried to email you several times. Please check your trash. Muchas gracias, Maria.' Within minutes Betty emailed back. 'I don't see anything from Estrella. Be sure she has my email address correct. Merci, Betty.'

We've all done it, sent to the incorrect email thinking we had the correct email. Anyway, Estrella sent Betty her original email requesting a meeting to see the wall space. Again, within minutes Betty responded, 'I'll be in New York next week. I'll have you stop by, look at the empty space and we can discuss your commission.'

It was the oven of August. The streets became lava black top and the sidewalks hotter than beach sand. I felt nervous about meeting Betty. I'd never done a major commission before. I had no idea what to say much less what to charge. I knew I needed to ask Luna for advice. I thought I would bring her with me to the meeting.

I texted Luna and we met up after my shift at her apartment. Quintessential New York City twenty-first century interior décor, Luna's Hotel Allen apartment was a surround sound of bright and pastel colors. White futuristic marble floors and feng shui placed mirrors made all the colors pop. She still had the turquoise sofa but now had it accented with hot pink throw pillows.

As always Luna wielded her smartphone like Thor's hammer. It was her superpower. "So, what's up prima?" she jabbed without looking Estrella in the eyes. She was the queen of multitasking.

"I need your help. You're a marketing wizardess. I have a meeting on billionaire's row for a major commission. What do I charge?"

Prima, let the billionaire suggest a fee. If you suggest a fee, it will more than likely be too low. A million dollars to the super rich are like a dollar to us. How large is the space?"

"I don't know but I know it's large. Probably at least ten feet by ten feet."

"How long will it take you to paint that size?"

"I'd say about a month. I'm working thirty hours as a barista at Macy's Cellar."

"I didn't know you were working. What for?"

"I'm pay two rents through August."

"Why didn't you say something. Upbeat can reduce your rent."

"They can?"

"Yes, I told them you could afford the three thousand a month. Upbeat had to agree to subsidize a creative person to get the top floor."

"I didn't know that. You mean Upbeat can charge less?"

"You got it Prima. What can you afford not working at Macy's?"

"Uh, a thousand? Estrella questioned timidly.

"Done. Now you can work full time on the commission."

"Will you come with me to my commission appointment?"

"Not. you need to handle it. The super-rich don't like to deal with agents and managers. If you get them involved, they give it to one of their assistants to work out the details."

Episode 47

Estrella got stressed out before the commission meeting. She called me obsessively every day. We're friends, right? Sometimes just put up with the bullshit when a friend calls.

One evening after dinner we FaceTimed. After listening to her pouring out her guts, we experienced a wonderful moment of silence. Estrella gently broke the soundless magic.

"Señor Escritor please tell me, tell me the answer."

"I have one of my favorite quotes from the Swiss Psychiatrist Carl Jung. I'll email it."

"Read it to me right now. I need to know now."

"I'm emailing it now. I'll read it; you follow along."

Estrella opened her email. The subject line read: Carl Jung – Thinking with the Heart.

"Carl Jung describes an encounter with the Native American chief Ochwiay Biano (Mountain Lake) of the Taos Pueblo in New Mexico in 1932.

"*I was able to talk with him as I have rarely been able to talk with a European,*" Jung recalled ...

Chief Mountain Lake: *"See how cruel the whites look, their lips are thin, their noses sharp, their faces furrowed and distorted by folds. Their eyes have a staring expression; they are always uneasy and restless. We do not know what they want. We do not understand them. We think they are all mad."*

When Jung was asked why he thinks they are all mad, Mountain Lake replied, *"They say they think with their heads."*

"Why of course," said Jung. *"What do you think with?"*

Chief Mountain Lake: *Points to his heart!*

Estrella tossed, turned and ate chocolate all night. 'Chief Mountain Lake thinks with his heart,' she reflected. Estrella thought endlessly, 'what does think with the heart mean?' Sometimes Estrella gracefully enters the inner temple. The quiet place, the painting place. Maybe that's what Chief Mountain Lake meant.

By the time, Estrella got picked up by Betty Morgan's limo she had made up her mind. She decided to think with her heart during the negotiations. This way she figured she didn't need to think on her feet. 'I guess I need to stop thinking with the monkey mind and think with the heart,'

The Morgan's high-tech castle in the sky reeked of wealth. Their home had no insects. After the twenty-fifth floor, bugs died of altitude sickness. Betty greeted me and raved about my mom. They had become fast friends. They FaceTimed at least once a week since they met.

Betty guided Estrella to a massive dining room where one bare wall faced Central Park.

"What did you have in mind Betty?" Estrella nervously asked.

"I want one of your classic gargoyles with pastel pink, peach and lemon creatively placed."

Estrella was speechless. She left with a check for fifty thousand dollars, half down and half later when the painting was hung. On the ride back to Hotel Allen Estrella felt she had turned the corner. Maybe that feeling comes with thinking with the heart.

Estrella was on it. With no more Macy's Estrella focused her whole day around painting. Her focus included the Morgan commission and the Hole in the Wall Gallery opening. I didn't hear much over the next few weeks. I promised to make her NYC gallery debut. I made the last first opening in Brooklyn Heights. Unfortunately, or fortunately, Estrella's paintings were surreptitiously removed from the gallery.

Episode 48

Estrella prepared for the Hole in the Wall Gallery opening without the same anticipation and excitement she would have months ago. The fifty thousand dollars advance freed her up to create any way she wanted. She picked out four previously painted gargoyles for the Hole in the Wall, put them aside and turned all her attention to the Morgan commission.

Since the twenty-by-twenty size would not fit out of the Hotel Allen freight elevator, Estrella divided the painting into four ten by ten paintings. This required her to be precise. The lines and colors in one painting needed to align exactly with the other three. Planning was a must.

Estrella felt fortunate that Betty Morgan did not micromanage the commission. She put her faith in Estrella's talent. She didn't require any photos. She didn't request visits to Estrella's loft. She didn't email, call or text. Estrella took an imagination flight. She soared like a hawk. The paintings magically took shape. The years of painting supported her craft and allowed her creativity to be in the Tao.

Estrella always FaceTimed me at least once a week. When I didn't hear from her for two weeks, it was time for me to give her a call. Mostly I wrote in the morning after meditation and coffee. I only wrote about two hours a day, maybe three. I took lots of short breaks. You hear about writers writing all day. That's not me. I had a life outside of writing.

I knew that Estrella created differently. She painted like a hawk. She rode the air currents high overhead. When she spotted what needed to be painted, she painted feverishly in energy bursts. She didn't have a set routine like I did with writing. She waited patiently for the inspiration.

Episode 49

The Hole in the Wall Gallery opening came and went. Estrella sold one painting for a $1,000. The hot oven summer in NYC was financially rewarding.

For the first time since moving to New York Estrella felt like she turned the corner on establishing herself as a living, breathing, financially sound Manhattanite. Estrella felt so secure in her creative life she didn't even ask me to attend the Hole in the Wall. I offered. She let me know it was no big deal.

Estrella put the last stroke on the second canvas of the Morgan's giant gargoyle. She sat down opening her MacBook Pro. She checked her email. There was one from Betty Morgan. Estrella sent me a copy. It read.

Hi Estrella,

I have some exciting news. Your giant gargoyle, our giant gargoyle, will be the featured painting for the First Annual Guggenheim Museum Halloween Party this coming Halloween.

You will be the featured new artist.

All the best,

Betty

My phone rang seconds after Estrella forwarded the email. I was out walking by an iconic Maine harbor. I sat down on a bench, took a deep breath and cast my horizon eyes out into the Atlantic.

"What's up?" "Shit Señor, this is insane." Estrella spoke English more as a local now. "You know that commission I'm painting for the Morgans."

"Yeah."

`"It's going to hang in the Guggenheim for their Halloween party."

"Even though they haven't seen it?"

"It seems that way," Estrella answered with an element of doubt.

"That's unheard of. The Morgan's must have a lot of pull."

"They have a lot of money."

"Yes, they do. But it takes more than money to have that much pull at the Guggenheim," I rebutted.

"Has Betty seen anything?"

"Nothing. She's not a micromanager. All she has seen are the gargoyle paintings on my website."

"Be grateful. Appreciate your well-deserved good fortune."

"You've got to come. October thirty-first. Mark your calendar now. And Billy too."

"The social media and press coverage will be insane. You need some coaching. I'd listen to your LunaTicTok cousin."

"Yeah, you're right. If it hadn't been for her help on the website and finding the loft in Hotel Allen, where would I be?"

"If I recall she bought your first NYC painting. You may not like her, but she knows her shit."

"No shit!"

"You know what? I'll do an astrology chart for October thirty-first. It will give you some insight on what to expect and how to handle the Guggenheim gala."

"You, know how I feel about astrology. It's not my thing. You did do my chart for the best time to move to NYC and it seems like it's working out."

Episode 50

Estrella completed the Guggenheim gargoyle with time to spare. Her loft walls were not big enough to hang the four paintings to make one. To view how they looked together she laid them out on the floor and used a ladder to view from above. Separately the four paintings were nothing special. But when she laid them out something remarkable happened. The giant gargoyle came alive with dynamic awe.

Coordinating with Betty Morgan and the Guggenheim flowed with ease. They made all the arrangements to deliver and hang the paintings. Their service staff diligently coordinated and communicated with Estrella each step of the way. The Guggenheim public relations team set up the press, television and social media.

Estrella felt anxious. It was the kind of anxiety that most every performer feels before going out on stage or on the playing field. We set up an astrology chart reading about Halloween. I called a few days before to give her the low down. Estrella was skeptical, as she should be. I treated astrology as a practical life tool used to help navigate life's terrain.

Here's a summary of what I said.

With the Sun in Scorpio transformations abound in work, relationships and health. You have Mars in Scorpio. Mars is action energy and when in Scorpio it is intense, driven to the edge and, at times, over the edge, obsessive.

Being a Libra, you prefer peace and harmony. Scorpio dances with emotional drama. Harmony, Libra, and disharmony Scorpio can clash. You need to use your Moon Capricorn qualities to handle the unexpected and the serendipity. Moon Capricorn brings problem solving skills to the impossible. As a Libra, friendships provide organic assistance. Listen to those close to you. They will provide useful solutions.

Estrella took everything with a grain of salt. She agreed. She needed to use her Moon

Capricorn energy to keep problem-solving the unfolding of The Guggenheim Halloween Party. Basically, Estrella thought it as 'here's the situation. How are you going to handle it?'

That she did. She sipped a lot of cortados over the next few weeks. I didn't realize how much detail goes into preparing and showing art. I'm a writer; I write. I really don't see all that goes into it. I enjoy writing. It releases a kind of hug feeling energy field in, around and through. I'm assuming Estrella felt similar about her art.

I made my plans to come down to The City the day before Halloween. As usual I'd be staying with Billy in Brooklyn. I needed to come up with a costume. Billy planned on being the Hunchback of Notre Dame, again. Estrella was a gargoyle last year and no doubt would be a gargoyle again.

Estrella and I didn't talk much the week before the Halloween opening. She was the featured artist. In fact, she was the only artist featured. I found myself bragging and boasting about Estrella. The New York Times included the Halloween gala in the Arts & Entertainment section. They touted it as the Halloween Trick or Treat of the decade.

Estrella's photos painted social media, not to mention press media. I shared with my friends on Facebook and Instagram. When I met a friend for coffee, I brought my copy of The New York Times Arts & Entertainment section so I could show off. I was ordinarily proud of my bestie. Our love felt safe and sound and all tucked in.

Estrella really didn't like the limelight. She'd rather paint in shadows. The publicity distracted her. In high school Estrella was voted Most Creative her first three years. Her Senior year she asked her friends to not vote for her. It was someone else's turn she felt. She still came in third.

Episode 51

Finally, the big day arrived. I'm a writer. Can I start with "the big day arrived?" Boring! I need to come up with something else. How about? It was Estrella's Millennium Day! That might be too much. Nonetheless, all those who loved Estrella were excited.

Estrella arrived in her gargoyle costume in the Morgan limousine. As the limo pulled up to the Guggenheim behind a long line of limousines, Estrella put on the gargoyle mask and horns. Her gargoyle was vicious and benign simultaneously. Pure evil had no place in Estrella's world. To her, there was beauty in ugliness.

As a gargoyle Estrella emerged from the limo; the master of ceremonies announced her arrival.

"Ladies and gentlemen, our featured artist displaying a twenty-by-twenty painting titled – Gargoyle's Pink Light. Estrella! As the MC exhaled the cold air smoked from his mouth. The audience was mostly inside. But there were a few hundred costumed Halloween revelers taking in the pomp even though there was little ceremony. The freezing quartet played familiar scary movie themes like the themes from *Jaws, The Exorcist* and *Halloween*.

Estrella was greeted at the entrance by Betty Morgan and the museum director. Señor, that's me, and Billy were her guests. We were there to assist and to support Estrella. A thousand Halloween costumed revelers packed the giant Guggenheim main floor. The museum director guided Estrella along with myself and Billy to the Green Room. The giant main room space dominated Gargoyle's Pink Light.

We settled into the peace and quiet of the Green Room. Here was a sanctum away from the avalanching crowd cascading through the Guggenheim. There were Zabar goodies galore including a giant charcuterie. Estrella wasn't hungry. Billy and I were famished. We toasted, recognizing Estrella's leading role. The champagne bubbled on to our palates. Estrella loved champagne. To me it tasted like sugar water. It was an honored tradition.

Recharged, we donned our masks. Estrella readied herself internally for Halloween celebrity status. Just then there was door pounding. It wasn't a polite knock. It was more like let me in right now. Billy opened the door. Luna burst in carrying an outfit.

"You're wearing this. Nobody will recognize you wearing a gargoyle costume. You need to shine. This is your public relations going out party. Thousands of photographs will appear on social media tonight. You want people to recognize you. Guys, give us some privacy," Luna commanded.

Billy and I stationed ourselves below the Gargoyle's Pink Light. The social media gathered into a storm of smartphone cameras. Estrella materialized from the Green Room as if from a Star Trek transporter. Her radiance dazzled the crowd. The only other time I experienced Estrella's high frequency radiant presence was the first time I laid eyes on her at the Aqueduct Café.

Luna truly knew her social media. Right, she was. Lights, action camera swept across the main room. Internally, Estrella felt a bit unnerved. Externally, she appeared natural and confident. Without being overly narcissistic, Estrella radiated beauty.

Episode 52

The reveling spooked of an evil Halloween. My smartphone vibrated. I pulled it out of my pocket and looked. "Please Call Me." It was mama, Estrella's mother. I made sure Billy had my back and excused myself.

The Green Room radiated quiet calm. I called mama.

"Hi, it's Señor. What's happening?"

"Papa died. You need to tell Estrella."

"I'm so sorry for your loss. I promise I will let Estrella know as soon as I can."

Mama had no time for a goodbye. And I had no time to lose letting Estrella know. For a second, I thought about waiting until tomorrow. I dismissed that as not wise. As soon as possible made the most sense.

I headed back to the Gargoyle's Pink Light where Estrella was doing supermodel duty. I noticed Estrella whisper into Billy's ear. I didn't find out until sometime later she whispered, "Do you want to go for coffee some time?" Billy's head nodded.

I made eye contact with Estrella. She read me. We 'need to talk' darted out of my mind and eyes. The crowd was relentless. We nudged our way to the Green Room. I told her. An emotional nuke rippled exploded inside Estrella.

Before she could call mama Betty entered. Betty demanded Estrella pay attention.

"Your mama let me know about your papa. My limo is parked out front. He will drive you to our private jet. Señor, you need to go too. Do you have your passports?"

"I have mine. I bring it whenever I visit the city. I doubt Estrella has hers."

Luna barged into the Green Room waving a passport. She had gone to Hotel Allen, used a master key to enter Estrella's artist loft and rummaged through draws. She handed it to Señor.

The 767 mansion in the sky carried us toward Madrid. Estrella agonized. There's a tear in the aura when someone close dies. An unimaginable pain clutches with an iron hand.

We landed in Madrid and switched to a small private jet for the less than an hour flight to Segovia. I'm not going to give the play by play from here. You've seen so many stories you can write your own ending.

The New York media dramatized, magnified and stretched the facts. Estrella sprung into the New York City pantheon of heroes and heroines. Estrella could care less. She really didn't follow her press, tv and social media. I took a quick look at my smartphone before we landed in Segovia. A viral explosion of Estrella photos and likes dominated the next several NYC news cycles.

Estrella and I are kindred souls, good friends. We may even be from the same group soul. I had a high school history teacher ask the class, "what will last beyond this course?' No one really tried to guess. He answered his own question with a wise confidence, "friendship, friendship can last a lifetime. This course will last just one school year."

He often let us talk without saying a word. Other teachers usually told us to stop talking. He eventually did in his own unassuming way. He waited for the peak talk crescendo. At that point he followed up by saying, "only thing about friends, you need to not sabotage or enable each other. Support each other to be the best you can be." I can say without a doubt I have always support my friend who paints gargoyles, Estrella.

THE END

ESTRELLA PAINTS GARGOYLES – PARIS in 2026

Estrella Paints Gargoyles available on Kindle Vella.
Read first 10 Episodes Free.
Google: Kindle Vella. Enter Title. Read.

Spiritual Frequencies Online Academy – Where you
can become a Patreon for a modest monthly
subscription. Hundreds of Posts. Go to
Patreon.com/spiritualfrequencies

Email: spiritualfrequenciesonline@gmail.com
Instagram: drgfrequencies
YouTube: Greg Nielsen@DrG

Venmo: contribute directly to Conscious Books &
Spiritual Frequencies Online Academy @Greg-
Nielsen-9